The Wit and Wisdom

of

Jack Vance*

* as experienced by

Miguel Lugo

AuthorHouse™
1663 Liberty Drive
Bloomington, IN 47403
www.authorhouse.com
Phone: 1-800-839-8640

First published by AuthorHouse 1/24/2011

ISBN: 978-1-4520-9630-8 (sc)

Printed in the United States of America

This book is printed on acid-free paper.

Certain stock imagery © Thinkstock.

This book is dedicated to

Javi

"This is all your doing, you know."
(Ullward's Retreat)

Table of Contents

An Enhanced Flavor   1

Chapters

  1. "Words are what magic is made of!"   3
  2. "I wasn't listening"   7
  3. "Bad manners"   11
  4. " * "   17
  5. "I probably meant something else"   23
  6. "An open vocabulary"   29
  7. "Docking the boat"   37
  8. "An inkling of 'why' "   41
  9. "The quiet area"   47
10. "Change utterly!"   55
11. "I shall refrain from thinking"   61
12. "Throw away the cork"   67

Cover illustration by Ricardo Lugo, M.D.

An Enhanced Flavor

"My name is Teehalt, Lugo Teehalt. Will you drink?"
(Star King; I)

Well, my *name is Lugo, and I am an ardent fan of the works penned by Jack Vance. They are a permanent, integral part of my Life in Fiction.*

Consider watching a movie. The first time you see it, your attention is mostly caught up in the plot; that is, what is happening at the moment. If you see it a second time then, since you know what will happen, you start noticing small details; although they may not be crucial to the development of the plot, they still enhance the movie-watching experience by bringing added depth to the story.

And that's how Vance's books excel: his Science Fiction and Fantasy stories are my favorite books to read over and over. I lose myself in the richness of language, the depth of the descriptions, and the convolutions of the dialogue, each reading becoming a new experience – an enhanced flavor, if you will.

And what delicious dialogue! I often wish, coming upon a particularly enjoyable rejoinder, that I could speak like one of his characters. Hoping I could one day use some of these phrases in conversation, I began to mark those passages that would strike me as singular or notable.

"On what grounds?"
"Caprice," said Sir Estevan. "That's as good a reason as any."
(The Dogtown Tourist Agency; VII)

Before long, like many fans of his work, I had a large collection of favorite phrases that I would point to when asked why I liked Vance's books so much. This book that you hold in your hands is the logical result.

And yet a book of quotes, haphazardly put together, might fail to capture interest. I decided to organize them into broad categories of my own choosing.

"Your opinions of course carry great weight," said Efraim."
(Marune: Alastor 933; VIII)

So you may find them yourself, these passages are identified by the story they were taken from and the chapters in which they appear.

1

"Any questions?"

No one spoke.

Henry Belt nodded. "Wise. Best not to flaunt your ignorance so early in the game." (Sail 25; 1)

I often think Vance somehow speaks to me on a personal level. For example, his is the only SF book I know of that has a character named Lugo. That must count for something, no?

"Come now," said Gersen lightly. "A name is no more than a word." (The Face; VII)

*I am a physician, an ophthalmologist, and his works contain multiple references to eyes and vision. Some examples are the magic cusps of **The Eyes of the Overworld**, the Optidynes of **The Languages of Pao**, and the "pumps" in **Cholwell's Chickens**.*

"Now, tincture of foxglove, to sparkle your eyes!" (Suldrun's Garden; VII)

I love Opera and I'm not aware of any other SF book, other than Vance's, whose main plot revolves around it.

"Whatever they call the racket, we can't have it disturbing everybody aboard." (Space Opera; VII)

And I play the accordion!

"Meanwhile, the accordionist plays another tune, and demands a tip."

"We will watch out for accordion-players or any other such rascals," said Maloof. (Ports of Call; V, 1)

I therefore decided to make this a very personal book: an exploration of my life reading speculative fiction, and how I came to discover these wonderful works. Your reading voyage was undoubtedly different from mine, but I trust you will also enjoy reliving the times you first encountered these flavorful quotations.

"I'd like it even more if you would fix the windows and splash on some paint." (Night Lamp; VI, 1)

Oh, well...

"Words are what magic is made of!"

Chapter one

Like most nearsighted kids, I was a voracious reader. Isaac Asimov once wrote that, as with any other innate ability, reading skills can be trained; the more you do it then the easier it becomes, the faster we do it and the better we can grasp the meaning of the words being examined.

*I must have been born with that talent, because I've been reading since I can remember. It served me well in school, where my best subject was Science. In Middle school my favorite books were the **Time-Life Nature Library** series (which I essentially memorized, becoming a young zoologist) and **The Adventures of Tintin** (my first graphic novels).*

In my hometown of Aguadilla, Puerto Rico, there were no bookstores in the 60s, so I had to patiently wait for my parents to make one of their uncommon trips to San Juan and bring me back a book of each series. They were quickly read a few times, soon memorized, and then the waiting would begin again.

*One day Mamá dragged me to the town's supermarket and it was there that I made a discovery that defined my reading tastes forever. On a revolving metallic display I saw a book with a giant spider in its cover, and a man under it defending himself with a pin. The year was 1971, I was 13 years old, and the book was **The Shrinking Man** by Richard Matheson.*

*Adventure and Science together in one story? What was this astonishing discovery I had made? Although this meant that I had to read a book in untranslated English, I couldn't resist it. My imagination was set on fire and, from that time on, I never complained about going to the supermarket. I went back to that wondrous revolving metal display and bought my second book, **A Mission of Gravity** by Hal Clemens. By now I was hopelessly hooked.*

*Other books soon followed: **Secret of the Sunless World** by Carroll M. Capps, **Skylark DuQuesne** by E.E. "Doc" Smith, **Recall not Earth** by C.C. MacApp...*

And thus a life in Science Fiction began.

*One day I was thrilled to find, in the magazine section, a copy of a monthly periodical called Fantasy and Science Fiction. It was the July 1971 issue and it featured Roger Zelazny's **Jack of Shadows**. I loved the magazine and immediately subscribed to it. Do you remember Gahan Wilson's cartoons?*

Then the fateful July 1972 issue of F&SF arrived, serializing a book by an author new to me. It was **The Brave Free Men** *by Jack Vance.*

Although I was catching the story in the middle, as this was the second book in the Durdane series, I quickly fell under the spell of this masterful storyteller. And what an abundance of unusual words I found in this book! Allow me to show you some of them:

"I hope that you have profited by your rest?"

"Such profits are **brummagem**," snapped Frolitz. "The troupe **rusticates**." (The Brave Free Men; VI)

"How far?"

"Two miles."

"Order a **diligence**." (The Brave Free Men; IV)

Diligence *I could figure out because of the Spanish word* diligencia, *or stage coach. But* **brummagem** *and* **rusticates**? *Some of these words weren't even in my paperback edition of the Merriam-Webster!*

"The first element is as I have *adumbrated*." (Ports of Call; II, 2)

"You said I played like a drunken squirrel."

"Yes, I remember the occasion. You used a clumsy vibrato. In the attempt for sentiment you achieved only *larmoyance*." (The Book of Dreams; XIII)

With a languid step he approached the table. "Hard at your *lucubrations*, so I see." (Araminta Station; IV, 3)

Callou studied the clerk with intense concentration, eyes bulging, cheeks puffed out. "You were motivated to this deed by your native altruism?"

"There was a small *emolument* involved. Nothing of an irregular sort." (Throy; V, 6)

I have transgressed, but so I justify my *peccancies*." (Ecce and Old Earth; I, 1)

"Well spoken!" declared Philidor. "But let me *propound* a parable." (The Last Castle; III, 2)

Casmir ignored the gibes, which exaggerated his appetites; indeed, he was almost austere in his use of *catamites*. (The Green Pearl; VIII, 3)

Kalash gave his black beard a defiant tug. "I am not a man who *tergiversates*!" (Ports of Call; IV, 4)

4

And let us not forget what may be the most-often quoted unusual word in his work!

"...and while the subject is fresh in my mind, I would like you to resolve a perplexity. A single father often boasts four sons, but how does a single son boast four fathers?"

Dissrel, Vasker and Archimbaust rapidly tapped the table; the eye, ear and arm were interchanged. At last Vasker made a curt gesture. "The question is *nuncupatory.*" (Cugel's Saga; VI, 1)

*Sometimes he borrows words from the Spanish or French, such as **diligence**, **frisson** (Night Lamp; XV, 1), **sacerdote** (The Dragon Masters; II) and **escritoire** (Bad Ronald; VIII); other times he just makes them up:*

'*Bouschterness*,' untranslatable, is roughly equivalent to 'conspicuous vulgarity' or 'obviously absurd and unsuitable display' such as wearing an expensive garment at an inappropriate occasion, or flaunting extravagant ornaments. (Throy; Glossary A*)*

But lest the reader get the impression that Vance's stories are stilted or falsely-erudite, let me quickly deny this. These words add immensely to the enjoyment of the story. Richard Tiedman, in discussing Jack Vance's style, tells us:

How does Vance's style differ from that of others? First, in his use of uncommon words; the stories are bedecked with rare words, exotic idiom, and rich texture. The unusual word (unusual to spoken conversation) is used to produce the utmost variety of color and effect.... Besides, how much more elegant to be "subaqueated" rather than drowned. (Writers of the 21st Century Series: Jack Vance, Taplinger Publishing Co., New York, 1980; p. 182)

He seized her, dragged her to the vacated box, locked her within; then returning to the console, pressed home the fire-valve, and the priestess sang an ululating contralto. (City of the Chasch; V)

Much more elegant indeed to "sing an ululating contralto" than to "scream"!

*And so **The Brave Free Men** was my happy introduction to Jack Vance, exotic words and all. Do these unusual words truly help him to tell his stories? Let his characters answer the question:*

Palafox interrupted incisively. "Words are tools." (The Languages of Pao; IX)

"Words are the vehicle of ideas. Ideas are the components of intellectualization." (The Gray Prince; II)

"You have been scrupulous in the choice of your words; it is a trait I appreciate." (Maske:Thaery; XX)

"Words are without substance."
"Wrong!" declared Tippin with intense fervor. "Words are what magic is made of!" (The Face; VII)

"I wasn't listening"

Chapter two

The Brave Free Men left me wanting for more, but I would have to wait until the May 1973 issue of Fantasy & Science Fiction before I could read the final book in the Durdane series, The Asutra. Meanwhile, an advertisement in the F&SF magazine allowed me to increase the number of books I could read: I joined the Science Fiction Book Club.

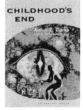

*I took advantage of the initial offer of 5 books for $1 and ordered what many consider to be classics of the genre: **Childhood's End** by Arthur C. Clarke, and **Ringworld** by Larry Niven.*

*I also ordered **The Hugo Winners**, which happily included two stories by Jack Vance: **The Dragon Masters** and **The Last Castle**.*

In these two stories the lead character must question the status quo and challenge the authorities that, unwilling or unable to change, constantly thwart his efforts. Being a young teenager, this rebellious attitude resonated within me.

"If your theory is accurate – and I pass no immediate judgement – then perhaps I would be wise to take similar measures. But I think in different terms. I prefer attack, activity, to passive defense."

"Admirable," said Joaz Banbeck. "Important deeds are done by men such as you." (The Dragon Masters; IV)

And although there is plenty of action in Jack Vance's stories, the "action" I enjoy the most is this verbal to-and-fro: the quick sardonic, ascerbic remark and its counterattacking, withering response.

Delfin cried out: "Egalism is envied across the cluster! Since all Alastor cannot come to Arrabus, then egalism must be spread across the Cluster. This should be your immediate duty!"

The Connactic showed the trace of a somber smile. "I must study your ideas with care. At the moment their logic eludes me." (Wyst: Alastor 1716; I)

Breaugh made an impatient gesture. "Very true. But that's a side issue to the idea I was trying to develop." (Chateau D'If; I)

Myrus the Mneidoes, an old man, thin and small, withered and sallow, was third in precedence. He spoke in a husky voice: "The idea of 'change' had occurred to many people; therefore we must be ready to accept 'change' as an accomplished fact. This seems to be your position: sheer nonsense, of course. Lust and envy obsess many of us; do we therefore legitimize these impulses? Our ancient creed is correct. Rather than submitting to change we must divert the influences which conduce in such a direction."

Ramus Ymph listened with patient good humor. "The remarks of the sagacious Servant are persuasive, even though they fail to correspond with reality." (Maske:Thaery; III)

Eyvant raised his eyebrows. "You do not respond amiably to censure."

"Censure should be based upon understanding of the facts, not an automatic outcry." (Maske:Thaery; VII)

"Never have I heard such nonsense," declared Wingo. "At least, not since your last harangue." (Ports of Call; VI)

Responses need not be aggressive; a subtle word or phrase can derail an opponent's expostulation. One of my favorites (and this one I have actually used!) is the first of the following excerpts:

Magnus Ridolph scanned the chart, glanced up into Thifer's big flat face. "Clearly I am dense. You have spoken at length and I still fail to understand your problem." (Magnus Ridolph: To B or not to C or to D)

"Have I heard rightly? You intend that I should descend into the hole? The idea lacks merit." (Madouc; II, 4)

"Your opinions are not as absorbing as you may believe." (Maske:Thaery; VII)

"That is a fine analogy," said Pirie Tamm. "Its only fault is unintelligibility." (Ecce and Old Earth; VII, 1)

"Your points are well-taken," said Efraim. "I could not dispute them if they were not founded upon incorrect premises." (Marune: Alastor 933; VI)

"No doubt you're right," he said, "although I don't understand the immediate relevance." (StarKing; VII)

8

Not always do the characters engage in discussion. Sometimes they simply find ways around the verbal confrontation, as in these examples:

"Do not be fooled by Ashgale! The opportunities he offers are worthless!"

Viliweg uttered a jeering laugh. "Can you offer better?"

"The question is sterile," said Zamp. (Showboat World; VI))

Dame Hester studied Dame Betka with somber calculation. "I am not one to intrude upon another's secrets, so I will ask you no further questions."

"I am glad to hear this," said Dame Betka. "You would only find my responses exasperating." (Ports of Call; I, 5)

"In all candor, I cannot understand why a scholar of your credentials should be traveling to Kyril, like one of the pilgrims, and presumably planning to join the march around the continent. Can you explain?"

"Naturally," said Cuireg with a cool smile. "However, I do not propose to do so, since you would surely find the ideas abstract, and probably beyond your comprehension." (Lurulu; XI, 4)

These last excerpts show us what may be the ultimate way of winning a discussion: disregard it!

Ildefonse asked: "Lehuster, is this your concept of a 'terse statement' in response to my question? First rumor, then speculation, then scandal and bias?"

"For the sake of clarity perhaps I overshot the mark," said Lehuster. "Also - in all candor - I have forgotten your question." (Rhialto the Marvellous; I, 2)

Gerd Jemasze spoke to no one in particular. "I won't say that all this talk is a waste of time, because people seem to enjoy it." (The Gray Prince; II)

Julian performed an airy flourish of the wine glass. "In a world of infinite choices, anything is possible. All things flow. Nothing is fixed."

Lewyn Barduys looked at Flitz. "Julian is talking high abstraction! Are you confused?"

"No."

"Ah! You are acquainted with these ideas?"

"I wasn't listening." (Ecce and Old Earth; I, 5)

"Bad Manners"

Chapter Three

When I joined the Science Fiction Book Club in 1972 I was a Sophomore at Bishop McManus Catholic High School. Having grown up in a predominantly Catholic island, and being subjected to the priests and nuns' legendary discipline, I had little cause to doubt or challenge their religious teachings.

Over the years my views on organized religion shifted considerably, in no little part because of SF stories I read.  ***A Canticle for Leibowitz*** *by Walter M. Miller first made me question how Catholicism may have changed over the centuries, perhaps mutating dramatically from its initial tenets.* ***A Case of Conscience*** *by James Blish postulated whether our religions would even be relevant to beings in other planets. And who can forget Zelazny's "Agnostic prayer" in Creatures of Light and Darkness?*

But before I read any of these books I encountered the "sacerdotes" (Spanish for "priests") in **The Dragon Masters**. *This cult of religious people profess non-interference in the affairs of others, yet suddenly take an active role when they themselves are threatened and so prove to be instrumental in the resolution of the conflict.*

Reading Vance's stories we often encounter skepticism or even cynicism regarding the officers or leaders of organized religions:

"Are you yourself a Christian?"

The young man made a negative sign. "The concepts of religion baffle me."

"This inscrutability is perhaps not unintentional," said the ex-priest. "It gives endless employment to dialecticians who otherwise might become public charges or, at the very worst, swindlers and tricksters." (The Green Pearl; I, 4)

The thrifty Soumi reasoned that a credo purporting to provide enlightenment must be readily comprehensible; if expensive specialists were needed for interpretation, the doctrine must be considered unsuitable and impractical. One of the elders deputed to select an optimum doctrine was blunt, averring that 'only fools would hoist a

religion upon themselves which cost them their hard-earned money."
(Throy; Glossary A)

"To the right is Saint Sophia's Cathedral with nineteen domes. At the center is Saint Andrew's Church of eleven domes, and to the left is Saint Michael's Monastery, with only nine domes. The cathedral and the church are lavishly decorated with mosaics, statues and other bedizenment of gold and jewels. Old Kiev suffered many devastations, and Kolsky Square has witnessed many awful incidents. But today, visitors from across the Gaean reach come only to marvel at the inspiring architecture and at the power of priests who were able to wring so much wealth from a land at that time so poor." (Ecce and Old Earth; V, 3)

In poignant tones Kalash pleaded: "Think beneficially of us and our pilgrimage! Like the paladins of old, we are dedicated to deeds of glory! Our way is often stark, often bitter! Still as we traverse the wastes of Kyril, we shall acclaim the altruists who helped us along the way!"
Maloof chuckled. "We also pursue glorious goals, such as profit, survival, and the sheer joy of wringing revenue from parsimonious passengers."
"That is a crass philosophy!"
"Not so!" declared Maloof. "Rationality is never crass. It suggests that if you can afford the luxuries of an expensive religion, you can afford to pay full rate, plus all applicable surcharges on your baggage." (Ports of Call; IV, 1)

"Sacerdotal, religious or priest-dominated societies are like organisms with a cancer." (Night Lamp; XI, 2)

Vance satirizes the overly-elaborate rituals that often define religious beliefs. Although spiritual leaders may be sincere, what they say sounds ridiculous to us:

The elder pointed a long quivering finger through the gloom. "I thought to detect heretical opinion; now the fact is known! Notice: he sleeps with neither head-covering nor devotional salve on his chin. The girl Zhiaml Vraz reports that at no time in their congress did the villain call out for the approval of Yelisea!"
"Heresy beyond a doubt!" declared the others of the deputation.
"What else could be expected of an outlander?" asked the elder contemptuously. "Look! Even now he refuses to make the sacred sign."
"I do not know the sacred sign!" Cugel expostulated. "I know nothing of your rites! This is not heresy, it is simple ignorance!"
"I cannot believe this," said the elder. "Only last night I outlined the nature of orthodoxy."

"The situation is grievous," said another in a voice of portentous melancholy. "Heresy exists only through putrefaction of the Lobe of Correctitude." (The Eyes of the Overworld; IV)

"King Kragen is our benefactor! What is this foolish talk of risk and slavery and sacrifice? Instead we should speak of gratitude and praise and worship." (The Blue World; V)

"Why does he not participate in Soul Endowment? What of his Basic Saltations? He knows neither Rite nor Rote nor Doxology; nor Leaps nor Bounds! Finuka requires more than this!"
… "The lad is hardly old enough to think. If he has a mind to devotion, he'll know fast enough; then he'll more than make up for any lack."
The Leaper became excited. "A fallacy! Children are best trained young. Witness myself! When I was an infant, I crawled upon a patterned rug! The first words I spoke were the Apotheosis and the Simulations. This is best! Train the child young! As he stands now he is a spiritual vaccum, susceptible to any strange cult! Best to fill his soul with the ways of Finuka!" (Emphyrio; V)

Chilke nudged Glawen's elbow. "See yonder, the lady in black? She's a Mascarene! A long time ago one of them tried to convert me. Partly out of curiosity, and partly because – from what little I could see of her – I sensed youth, a comely exterior and an eager personality. I asked what was involved, and she said it was quite simple: first I must undergo the Seven Degradations, then the Seven Humiliations, then the Seven Penances, then the Seven Outrages, then the Seven Mortifications, and a few more activities which I've forgotten. At this time the acolyte was supposed to be in the proper frame of mind to become a good Mascarene, and go out to convert other like-minded souls and collect their money. I asked if she and I would undergo these rites in a close association, consulting during each degradation, but she said no, her grandmother would make this sacrifice. I told her that I would think things over, and there the matter rested." (Throy; II, 5)

It makes you wonder how much of our cherished personal rituals may ultimately prove to be no more useful than the Simulations or the Seven Mortifications…
At other times, the discussions turn philosophical, although pragmatism is often given the last word:

"As I see it, the cosmos is probably infinite, which means – well, infinite. So there are local situations – a tremendous number of them. Indeed, in a situation of infinity, there are an infinite set of local conditions, so that somewhere there is bound to be anything, if this anything is even remotely possible. Perhaps it is; I really don't know what the chances – "

13

"Come, come!" snapped the leader. "You are blithering! Declare us this dramatic enlightenment in plain words!"

"Well, it might be that in certain local regions, by the very laws of chance, a god like Finuka might exist and exert local control. Maybe even here, on the North Continent, or over the whole world. In other localities, gods might be absent. It depends, of course, upon the probability of the particular kind of God." Ghyl hesitated, then added modestly, "I don't know what this is, of course."

The leader drew a deep breath. "Has it occurred to you that the individual who attempts to reckon the possibility or probability of a god is puffing himself up as the spiritual and intellectual superior of the god?"

"No reason why we can't have a stupid god," muttered Nion Bohart..." (Emphyrio; VII)

Wingo was greatly interested in comparative metaphysics: the sects, superstitions, religions and transcendental philosophies that he inevitably encountered as the Glicca traveled from world to world endlessly fascinated him. Whenever he wandered strange places, he gave careful attention to local spiritual doctrines: a practice that aroused Schwatzendale's disapproval. "You are wasting your time! They all talk the same nonsense and only want your money. Why bother? Religious cant is the greatest nonsense of all!"

"There is much in what you say," Wingo admitted. "Still, is it not possible that one of these doctrines is correct and exactly defines the Cosmic Way? If we passed it by, we might never encounter Truth again."

"In theory, yes," grumbled Schwatzendale. "In practice, your chances are next to nil." (Ports of Call; IV, 2)

"My philosophy presupposes a succession of creators, each absolute in his own right. To paraphrase the learned Pralixus, if a deity is possible, it must exist! Only impossible deities will not exist! The eight-headed Zo Zam who struck off his Divine Toe is possible, and hence exists, as attested by the Gilfigite Texts!"

...Garstang, sitting to the side, smiled thoughtfully. "And you, Cugel the Clever, for once you are reticent. What is your belief?"

"It is somewhat inchoate," Cugel admitted. "I have assimilated a variety of viewpoints, each authoritative in its own right: from the priests at the Temple of Teleologues; from a bewitched bird who plucked messages from a box; from a feasting anchorite who drank a bottle of pink elixir which I offered him in jest. The resulting visions were contradictory but of great profundity. My world-scheme, hence, is syncretic."

"Interesting," said Garstang. "Lodermulch, what of you?"

"Ha," growled Lodermulch. "Notice this rent in my garment; I am at a loss to explain its presence! I am even more puzzled by the existence of the universe." (The Eyes of the Overworld; V, 2)

14

Not all religious discussions are meant to be ironic. I suspect the author's viewpoint can sometimes be gleaned through the words of these characters:

"Still, there is much that you do not know," said Reith. "In fact, nearly everything." (Servants of the Wankh; VI)

Anacho, still smarting from Reith's comparisons, looked across the deck. "Well then, what of Adam Reith, the erudite ethnologist? What theosophical insights can he contribute?"

"None," said Reith. "Very few, at any rate. It occurs to me that the man and his religion are one and the same thing. The unknown exists. Each man projects on the blankness the shape of his own particular world-view. He endows his creation with his personal volitions and attitudes. The religious man stating his case is in essence explaining himself. When a fanatic is contradicted he feels a threat to his own existence; he reacts violently." (Servants of the Wankh; III)

The Demie said mildly, "Facts can never be reconciled with faith." (The Dragon Masters; VI)

From Life, Volume 1 by Unspiek, Baron Bodissey:
If religions are diseases of the human psyche, as the philosopher Grintholde asserts, then religious wars must be reckoned the resultant sores and cankers infecting the aggregate corpus of the human race. Of all wars, these are the most detestable, since they are waged for no tangible gain, but only to impose a set of arbitrary credos upon another's mind. (The Face; III)

Hugh glared from his cavernous eye-sockets. "Are you admitting to atheism?"

"If you want to put it that way," said Don. "I don't see why you make it out a bad word. Atheism is the assertion of human self-reliance, dignity and individuality."

"You are forever damned," said Hugh in a hushed sibilant voice.

"I don't think so," said Don reasonably. "Of course I don't know anything for sure. No one knows the basic answers. Why is everything? Why is anything? Why is the universe? These are tremendous questions. They aren't answered by replying, 'Because the Creator so willed.' The same mystery applies to the Creator. I'm sure he's not angry when I use the brain and curiosity He endowed me with," said Don smiling. (Parapsyche; IV)

I'm sure that, indeed, the Creator is not. Still,

"Lesson number one in Earth culture," said Joe cheerfully. "It's bad manners to argue religion." (Son of the Tree; XII)

15

" ✲ "

Chapter Four

*Having read the two Hugo-winning stories, as well as the serialized versions of **The Brave Free Men** and **The Asutra**, I was eager to get my hands on other Jack Vance books. Unfortunately I would have to wait several years before I could do so.*

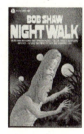 *Meanwhile I kept reading any SF books that made it to the revolving metal display, like Bob Shaw's **Nightwalk** and Ray Bradbury's **The Illustrated Man**. I always carried a paperback with me to school and surreptitiously read it while the class was going on. If called upon to answer a question, I usually had the right answer, so how could the teacher object?*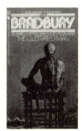

*Then came my "miracle summer" of 1973, during which I read, back-to-back, **Dune** and **The Lord of the Rings**; I don't think I ever quite recovered from that!*

*The next Jack Vance story I read was **The Dogtown Tourist Agency**, in the collection **Epoch** that the SF Book Club featured in May 1976. Although I had encountered footnotes in the other Vance books, there was one in this story that stuck with me:*

*SLU, Standard Labor-value Unit, the monetary unit of the Gaean Reach, defined as the value of an hour of unskilled labor under standard conditions. The unit supersedes all other monetary bases, in that it derives from the single invariable commodity of the human universe – toil. (The Dogtown Tourist Agency; II)

Up to this point I had read those previous footnotes and thought little of them. This particular one, however, posed a rather profound question: how to value human toil? And, given its value, what better monetary unit to employ?

*Zink, a coin representative of a man-minute, the hundredth part of an SLU. Gaean time is based upon the standard day of Earth, subdivided into twenty-four hours, after ancient tradition. A minute is the hundredth part of an hour, a second is the hundredth part of a minute. (The Dogtown Tourist Agency; VI)

17

These footnotes were to the story as icing to the cake![*]

The February 1977 selection of the SF Book Club was to be the first Vance novel I held in my hand: **Maske:Thaery**. To me this book would come to represent the quintessential Jack Vance story, with its exotic locales, conflicts of caste and societal discrimination, cultural and political conflicts resolved by the battle of wits... and, of course, footnotes galore! This one follows just after the second word of the novel:

*The conventions of galactic direction are like those of a rotating planet. The direction of rotation is east, the opposite west. When the fingers of the right hand extend in the direction of rotation, the thumb points to the north and opposite is south. "Inward" and "outward" refer to motion toward or away from the center of the galaxy. (Maske:Thaery; i)

Sometimes his footnotes are simple definitions:

*Strochane: a mythical being with supernormal powers, whose commands no mortal men can disobey. (Maske:Thaery; III)

Others were informative expositions of matters touched upon, but otherwise not explained, in the story:

*Numerous systems of chronometry create confusion across Alastor Cluster and the Gaean reach, despite attempts at reform. In any given locality, at least three systems of reckoning are in daily use: scientific chronometry, based upon the orbital frequency of the K-state hydrogen electron; astronomic time – 'Gaean Standard Time' – which provides synchronism across the human universe; and local time. (Marune: Alastor 933; I)

*The Djans weave rugs of unexampled splendor and intricacy. Ten Thousand knots per square inch is not unusual. The rugs are occasionally characterized as "one-life", "two-life," and so forth, to indicate the aggregate number of lifetimes invested in the creation of the rug. (Maske:Thaery; I)

*The use of footnotes was an early stylistic decision; I was able to find its first instance in **The Sub-Standard Sardines**, an early Magnus Ridolph*

---

[*] *I will now indulge in a footnote myself! Vance used 'SVU' in the earlier Demon Princes books, and defined it at the "Standard Value Unit of the Oikumene". It wasn't until **The Grey Prince** that he gave it the same definition as in **The Dogtown Tourist Agency** and tied its value to human toil. In **Freitzke's Turn**, published one year after, he reverted to SVUs instead of SLUs. In **Araminta Station** he defines the 'sol' in a similar fashion.*

story and his 8th published work. ♣ *Initially simple and short explanations, they eventually grew in length and complexity.*

*Trismet: The group of persons resulting from a 'trisme', the Rhune analog of marriage. These persons might be a man and his trismetic female partner; or a man, the female partner, one or more of her children (of which the man may or may not be the sire). 'Family' approximates the meaning of 'trismet' but carries a package of inaccurate and inapplicable connotations. Paternity is often an uncertain determination; rank and status, therefore, are derived from the mother. (Marune: Alastor 933; IV)

*Wittols: One of every thousand Uldras is born albino, eunuchoid, short of stature and round-headed. These are the wittols, treated with a mixture of repugnance, contempt and superstitious awe. They are credited with competence at small magic and witchcraft; occasionally they deal in spells, curses and potions. Major magic remains the prerogative of the tribal warlocks. The wittols bury dead, torture captives, and serve as emissaries between tribes. They move with safety across the Alouan, since no Uldran warrior would either deign or dare to kill a wittol. (The Gray Prince; I)

*Cultural psychologists have defined the symbology of 'wait-times' and its variation from culture to culture. The significance of the intervals is determined by a large number of factors, and the student can easily list for himself, out of his own experience, those which are relevant to his own culture.

'Wait-times,' in terms of social perception, range from no wait whatever to weeks and months. In one context a wait of five minutes will be interpreted as 'unpardonable insolence'; at another time and place a wait of only three days is considered a signal of benign favor.

The use of an exactly calculated 'wait-time', as every person familiar with the conventions of his own culture understands, can be used as an assertion of dominance, or 'putting one in one's place,' by legal and nonviolent methods.

The subject has many fascinating ramifications. For instance, Person A wishes to assert his superior status over Person B, and keeps him waiting an hour. At the thirty-minute mark, which B already feels to be unacceptable and humiliating, A sends B a small tray of tea and sweetcakes, a gesture which B cannot rebuff without loss of dignity. A thereby forces B to wait a full hour and B must also thank A for his graciousness and bounty in the matter of the inexpensive refreshments. When well-executed, this is a beautiful tactic. (Araminta Station; II, 9)

♣ *In this, as in other publishing details, I am indebted to Jerry Hewett and Daryl F. Mallett scholarly* **The Work of Jack Vance: An annotated bibliography and guide**, *Underwood-Miller, 1994.*

19

*Interestingly, it is in the even earlier Magnus Ridolph story **Hard-Luck Diggins** (5th published) that we see for the first time a related stylistic device: the preface. Here is what may be the most celebrated one of those in the Ridolph stories:*

Banish Evil from the world? Nonsense! Encourage it, foster it. The world owes Evil a debt beyond imagination. Think! Without greed ambition falters. Without vanity art becomes idle musing. Without cruelty benevolence lapses to passivity. Superstition has shamed man into self-reliance and, without stupidity, where would be the savor of superior understanding? (The Sub-Standard Sardines*)*

Richard Tiedman says:
What is interesting is the contrapuntal development of the narrative in conjunction with prefaces to the chapter... On the one hand, it provides a spotlight for throwing, from various angles, light on the multiple aspects of the society under study. Some of the prefaces are mere embellishment, without relation to the narrative proper; others are essential to a proper understanding of the plot. ◆

The prefaces came to a zenith in the Demon Princes books. Here we encounter excerpts from articles in magazines such as Cosmopolis, transcripts from speeches and political discourses, as well as authoritative works like Tourists guide to the Coranne, Popular Handbook to the Planets, The Demon Princes, and A Concise History of the Oikumene. Chapters often have a multi-page preface containing several of these references.

Unquestionably the highlights are the excerpts from Baron Bodissey's monumental multi-volume opus, Life, and the quotes and poems of the "Mad Poet" Navarth. Both of these fictional authorities become so real through these prefaces that they each have an entry in Wikipedia!

We've already encountered Unspiek, Baron Bodissey in the previous chapter, speaking about religious wars. Here, therefore, is one of Navarth's poems, whose multiple allusions to poisoning (Amanita mushrooms, botulinum bacteria, upas tree, sturgeon's roe, etc.) prepare us for what may soon transpire:

**Avris rara, black mascara
Will you stay to dine with me?
Amanita botulina
Underneath my upas tree.**

**This dainty tray of cloisonné
Contains my finest patchouli
Aha, my dear! What have we here?
A dead mouse in the potpourri.**

◆ *Jack Vance: Science Fiction Stylist, in **Writers of the 21st Century Series: Jack Vance**. Taplinger Publishing, N.Y. 1980, p. 213-214.*

With mayonnaise the canapés
Ravished from a sturgeon's womb;
With silver prong we guide along
The squeaking oyster to his doom.

A samovar of hangdog tea:
A cup, or are you able?
Antimony, macaroni
On my hemlock table.

-Navarth

(The Palace of Love; XIII)

But the prefaces that most intrigued me were those totally superfluous excerpts from "The Avatar's Apprentice", found towards the end of each Demon Prince book. They grow in length and complexity from **Star King** *(two paragraphs) to* **The Book of Dreams** *(five pages), and follow Marmaduke (the apprentice?) in his quest for enlightenment – or, at least, survival. So let's finish this chapter with my favorite one:*

Struggling to the hill's crest, Marmaduke searched for the blasted cypress which marked the hut of the symbologist. There stood the tree, haggard and desolate, and a hut nearby.

The symbologist gave him welcome. "A hundred leagues I have come," said Marmaduke, "to put a single question; Do the colors have souls?"

"Did anyone aver otherwise?" asked the perplexed symbologist. He caused to shine an orange light, then, lifting the swing of his gown, he cavorted with great zest. Marmaduke watched with pleasure, amused to see an old man so spry!

The symbologist brought forth green light. Crouching under the bench he thrust his head between his ankles and turned his gown outside to in, while Marmaduke clapped his hands for wonder.

The symbologist evoked red light, and leaping upon Marmaduke, playfully wrestled him to the floor and threw the gown over his head. "My dear fellow," gasped Marmaduke, winning free, "but you are brisk in your demonstration!"

"What is worth doing is worth doing well," the symbologist replied. "Now to expatiate. The colors admit of dual import. The orange is icterine humor as well as the mirth of a dying heron.

"Green is the essence of second-thoughts, likewise the mode of the north wind. Red, as we have seen, accompanies rustic exuberance."

"And a second import of the red?" Marmaduke asked.

The symbologist made a cryptic sign. "That remains to be seen, as the cat said who voided into the sugar bowl."

Amused and edified, Marmaduke took his leave, and he was quite halfway down the mountain before he discovered the loss of his wallet.

(The Palace of Love; XIV)

"I probably meant something else"

Chapter Five

A fantasy book got me into Medical School.

*In February of 1977 I visited Temple University Medical School in Philadelphia. During the interview I was asked what book I was presently reading. I explained that I liked SF and Fantasy and mentioned the last two I had read, Philip José Farmer's **To Your Scattered Bodies Go**, and Harlan Ellison's short story collection **Deathbird Stories**. I then mentioned how happy I was that **The Silmarillion** was to be posthumously*  *published, and the physician turned out to be a huge Tolkien fan! The formal interview then turned into a most friendly conversation.*

 I received notification of my acceptance within a month. Once The Silmarillion was published I bought it for my interviewer, who later became my Pathology teacher and mentor.

 *Sometime during that summer I obtained a copy of **The Dying Earth**. Reading about Jack Vance, I had come across many references to this book. It isn't often that an author's first published work is this seminal, but even a quick read will show us the characteristic Vancian treatment of the fantasy themes.*

 Robert Silverberg says about The Dying Earth Books:

> The stories, ingenious and seductive, are built almost entirely out of conflicts; the war of wits, the contests of sorcerers, the ferocious struggles of rival rogues; and while conflict has been a wellspring of fiction since at least The Iliad and The Odyssey, it also in this case reveals a singularly bleak world-view made more palatable only by the elegance of the prose in which it is set forth and the unfailing courtliness with which the murderous beings of the dying Earth address one another.[*]

---

[*] *Jack Vance: Science Fiction Stylist, in **Writers of the 21st Century Series: Jack Vance**. Taplinger Publishing, N.Y. 1980, p. 126.*

Here are some examples of this elegant prose:

Most strange, however, was the sky, a mesh of vast ripples and cross-ripples, and these refracted a thousand shafts of colored light, rays which in mid-air wove wondrous laces, rainbow nets, in all the jewel hues. So as Turjan watched, there swept over him beams of claret, topaz, rich violet, radiant green. He now perceived that the colors of the flowers and the trees were but fleeting functions of the sky, for now the flowers were of salmon tint, and the trees a dreaming purple. The flowers deepened to copper, then with a suffusion of crimson, warmed through maroon to scarlet, and the trees had become sea-blue. (The Dying Earth: Turjan of Miir)

"This is an informal gathering; I will venture upon an unpleasant topic. The ordinary citizen of the Cluster shows a lack of self-consciousness regarding his bowel which is typically animal. Without shame he displays his victual, salivates, wads it into his orifice, grinds it with his teeth, massages it with his tongue, impels the pulp along his intestinal tract. With only little more modesty he excretes the digested mess, occasionally making jokes as if he were proud of his alimentary facility. Naturally we obey the same biological compulsions, but we are more considerate of our fellows and perform these acts in privacy." (Marune: Alastor 933; VII)

The Ninth Company presented a fête champêtre. In garments of pink and blue, green and blue, yellow and blue diaper, the players were engaging hybrids of fairies and harlequins. As before, there seemed no plot, no perceptible pattern of movement. The music was a chirping, twiddling, tinkling confection occasionally underscored by a hoarse booming like a foghorn's tone, or the blast of a conch. From side to side moved the players, this way and that: a pavanne? A bucolic celebration? The apparently aimless motion, the curtsies, the frivolous capering and cantering continued without development or alteration, but suddenly came the startling intuition that here was no farce, no gentle entertainment, but a presentment of something somber and terrible: an evocation of heart-rendering sadness. The lights faded to darkness. A flash of dazzling blue-green light revealed the Ninth Company in attitudes of attention and inquiry, as if they themselves were perplexed by the problem they had propounded. When the audience could see once more the curtain had fallen and the music had stopped. (SpaceOpera; I)

Water was considered an enervating, even despicable, fluid, to be shunned at all costs. No gypsy allowed himself or herself to be bathed, from infancy to death, for fear of rinsing away a magic personal unguent which, oozing from the skin, was the source of mana...

For an off-worlder to visit a Vongo encampment was, at any time, an unnerving experience, but the tribal camp meetings were even more intense. A favorite pastime of the young bucks was to kidnap and rape the girls of another tribe, which caused a great hubbub, but which seldom came to bloodshed, since such exploits were considered juvenile pranks, at which the girls had probably connived. A far more serious offense was the kidnap of a chief or a shaman, and the washing of him and his clothes in warm soapy water, in order to deplete him of his sacred ooze. After the washing, the victim was shorn of his beard and a bouquet of white flowers was tied to his testicles, after which he was free to slink back to his own tribe: naked, beardless, washed and bereft of mana. The wash water was carefully distilled, finally to yield a quart of yellow unctuous foul-smelling stuff, which would be used in tribal magic. (Night Lamp; I, 2)

To the first-time reader, Vance's language may seem to be overly-elaborate, perhaps a ruse or affectation. I, however, equate these descriptions to the overture of an Opera; not strictly necessary but often pivotal in setting the background and mood of the action to follow.

Verbal convolutions, however, are usually left to the characters and their struggles. Ask a question and you may not get a straight answer:

Panshaw's sensitive face became creased with perplexity. "You have surprised me; I need time to assess the situation."

"In short, you refuse to cooperate with me?"

"Please," murmured Panshaw. "Do not force unnatural meanings upon my remarks." (The Face; XIII)

"If folk want to exchange information, clarity is essential. If they want to confuse each other, various methods exist. They can use glossolalia, or a primitive language of clicks and grunts, or, as a last resort, the esoteric jargon of the Institute."

Cuireg was only mildly interested. "A pungent analysis. To what is it relevant?"

Wingo leaned back in his chair. "In regard to your visit to Kyril, you felt that your remarks would only confuse me. I suspect, however, that if you spoke in the ordinary gaean idiom, using standard syntax, I should be able to capture the gist of your remarks."

Cuireg was sardonically amused. "Take care, Wingo! The epistemological jungle is dark and deep! There are pitfalls and strange byways, and monsters lurk in the shadows. An intrepid traveler such as yourself, however, should manage to discover at least the basic dogma, which is starkly simple, and germane to our discussion; it asserts that between individuals, exact communication is never possible." He inspected Wingo. "You doubt the proposition? You need only refer to the physical laws of uncertainty – ignoring, of course, the mischievous corollary which states that the laws themselves are laughably uncertain!" (Lurulu; XI, 4)

Hachieri: Is it not true then that the Institute originated as a cabal of assasins?

Jesno: To the same degree that the Planned Progress League originated as a cabal of irresponsible seditionists, traitors, suicidal hypochondriacs.

Hachieri: This is not a pertinent response.

Jesno: The elasticities, the areas of vagueness surrounding the terms of your questions, do indeed encompass the exact truth of the situation. (The Palace of Love; X)

"Perhaps I am oversensitive, but it seems our relationship has not flowed as gracefully as I had hoped. I brought you a letter which you refused to read."

"Ah well, let us not mar the occasion with either recriminations or vain regrets." (Maske:Thaery; V)

"Ah yes! I now recall our meeting. Sir Denzel is a gentleman of distinction. I trust that his health is good?"

"As good as can be expected, when all is taken with all." (Throy; III, 2)

Sir Denzel is, of course, dead. Here are further examples of linguistic twists and turns:

"I bring you truth," announced Schwatzendale grandly. "Time and existence both lack Dimension! Life is real only during that instant known as 'Now'. Surely that is clear!"

"Oh, it is clear enough," scoffed Wingo. "You cite the most limpid banalities as if they were cosmic truths. For an unsophisticated person the effect might be startling"

Schwatzendale peered sidewise at the complacent Wingo. "You may or may not intend a compliment." (Ports of Call; VI)

"I was on the point of paying over sixty-five thousand sols into a special fund."

Glawen was astounded. "Sixty-five thousand sols from an account of twenty-nine thousand? That is a financial miracle!"

Chilke was not impressed and explained the mystery. "It is a special way of moving decimal points. Some bankers back home tried it, but they did not understand the system, so they were caught and sent to jail." (Throy; III, 2)

"Tomorrow," said Glawen, "I will be leaving early for Pogan's Point. You must sit in the lobby or in your room, but make sure the desk clerk knows where you are. If I am not back tomorrow evening, communicate with the IPCC. Did you hear me?"

Kirdy smiled: a curious smile, thought Glawen, of full poise and wisdom. "I heard your words. I understand them at all levels of my mind." (Araminta Station; VII, 5)

He may understand the words – but what is really being said?

"And when they catch their game?"
"The Dirdir are conservative. They do not recognize change," said Anacho. "They need not hunt but are driven by inner forces. They consider themselves beasts of prey, and impose no restraint upon themselves."
"In other words," said Traz, "they will eat us." (The Dirdir; II)

"Glyneth, I am a person who dances to a merry tune! Still, sometimes I must, by necessity and rightness, tread to a more portentous strain. I dislike excesses where events go wildly awry and affectionate trust is forever shattered. Do you apprehend my meaning?"
"You want me to obey you, and you promise me harm if I will not." (The Green Pearl; XV, 1)

"This is the meng. From one of his organs comes a substance which can be distributed either as ulgar or as furux. The same substance, mind you! But when sold as ulgar and administered as such, the symptoms are spasms, biting off of the tongue and a frothing madness. When sold and used as furux, the interskeletal cartilage is dissolved so that the frame goes limp. What do you say to that? Is that not metaphysics of the most exalted sort?"
"Interesting, certainly... Hm... What occurs when the substance is sold and used as, say for the sake of argument, water?"
Edelrod pulled at his nose. "An interesting experiment. I wonder... But the proposal encases a fallacy. Who would buy and administer an expensive vial of water?"
"The suggestion was poorly thought out," admitted Gersen. (The Palace of Love; II)

"Some of the material I will omit, for one reason or another, but I think you will find the balance interesting."
Dame Clytie instantly bristled. "Read the letter in its entirety, if you please. I see no reason for truncations. We are all either public officials or persons of the highest integrity."
Julian said gently: "Dear Aunt Clytie, I hope it is not a case of either one or the other." (Ecce and Old Earth; I, 5)

Myron asked in awe, "Where do you find such things?"
"The same place we find everything else! In ancient shrines, junk heaps, old ruins, excavations, private collections, native sources; in short, from anyone willing to sell or trade. Sometimes we find things

27

that no one seems to own, or so we hope, and we take them! That is known as 'dynamic scholarship'." (Ports of Call; VII, 1)

'Dynamic scholarship', otherwise known as 'theft!' Perhaps Norman Spinrad best defines the power of Vance's convoluted language when he says:
Whether he is describing an expiring millennial earth steeped in magic born of a rotting history, or a galactic cluster of 30,000 stars, or the planet Aerlith under the baleful eye of the wandering lizard star, Vance creates baroque tapestry.*

"First I must ensure that, once at liberty, you conduct yourself with unremitting loyalty, zeal and singleness of purpose."
"Have no fear," declared Cugel. "My word is my bond."
"Excellent!" cried Iucounu. "This knowledge represents a basic security which I do not in the least take lightly. The act now to be performed is doubtless supererogatory." (The Eyes of the Overworld; I)

I am a legalist and a financial expert, I admit as much; but my disregard for the law goes no further." (The Face; VI)

"The question is many-sided," said Etzwane. (The Brave Free Men; XIV)

"My daughter Wayness saw something of Julian on Earth. His conduct was not the best, and she has nothing good to say of him."
"I am not surprised, and I very much hope that he stays on Earth, since I prefer his absence to his company." (Throy; I, 3)

Lyssel's mouth drooped piteously. "But I thought that you wanted us to become friends!"
Jaro grinned. "I might have used the word, but I probably meant something else." (Night Lamp; VIII, 3)

---

* *Jack Vance: Science Fiction Stylist, in **Writers of the 21st Century Series: Jack Vance**. Taplinger Publishing, N.Y. 1980, p. 16.*

28

"An open vocabulary"

Chapter Six

*August of 1977 saw me moving to Philadelphia to begin my Medical education. The very same day my parents and I arrived in Philadelphia I dragged them to see **Star Wars**, a movie I had read about in Time Magazine. Although I was blown away by it, my father wasn't too impressed; he said it was little different from the **Buck Rogers** serials he had seen so many years before!*

And, although school was challenging, I still found time to continue 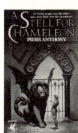 *reading SF and finding new authors. After all, I finally lived in a city that had bookstores! A few of the books that I remember reading then were the beginnings of some of my favorite series: Piers Anthony's **A Spell for Chameleon** and Stephen Donaldson's **Lord Foul's Bane**.*

I seemed to be caught in "series-madness", as that Fall I bought **Marune: Alastor 933**. *As had previously happened with the Durdane Series, and would also happen with the Demon Princes and Tschai: Planet of Adventure, I started to read midway through the Alastor series. Thankfully this was a complete stand-alone novel and required no previous information to understand the plot.*

As a burgeoning doctor I was amused by this quote from a physician, examining the main character who had lost his memory:

"I've never come in contact with such a case before. Fascinating! It's almost a shame to cure you!" (Marune: Alastor 933; II)

The story revolves around the protagonist's struggle to regain his identity. Although certainly capable of taking direct action or performing daring deeds, Vance's characters most often initially resort to combat using words:

Paul considered. He entered arguments only when he knew he could win them. Always, before committing himself, he made a careful mental reconnaissance. In this case he could see a clear and cogent continuity of ideas. He decided to argue. He would force Jim Connor to back away, to acknowledge him powerful, distinct, singular... (The House on Lily Street; VII)

Lorcas grinned and leaned forward. Here was the milieu he loved: conversation! Supple sentences, with first and second meanings and overtones beyond, outrageous challenges with cleverly planned slip-points, rebuttals of elegant brevity; deceptions and guiles, patient explanations of the obvious, fleeting allusions to the unthinkable. As a preliminary, the conversationalist must gauge the mood, the intelligence, and the verbal facility of the company. To this end a few words of pedantic exposition often proved invaluable. (Marune: Alastor 933; VII)

This concept of language as a tool is so important to Vance that he even wrote a novel where he explored the power it has to shape people's minds and actions:

"Think of a language as the contour of a water-shed, stopping flow in certain directions, channeling it into others. Language controls the mechanism of your mind. When people speak different languages, their minds work differently and they act differently." (The Languages of Pao; VIII)

"Words are tools. Language is a pattern, and defines the way the wordtools are used." (The Languages of Pao; IX)

Now who wouldn't want to command the English language well enough to engage in debates like these?

Etzwane said, "Your conduct is incomprehensible. Why did you assert that you could not take us to Caraz?"

"I made no such assertion," said Ifness. "You drew a faulty inference, for which I cannot accept responsibility. In any event the situation is more complicated than you suppose, and you must be prepared for subtlety."

"Subtlety or deception?" demanded Etzwane. "The effect is much the same." (The Asutra; II)

The captain attempted a final defiance. "You expect me to deliver our impregnable Kaul Bocach into your hands without as much as a protest?"

"Protest all you like. In fact, I'll let you go back within. Then you are under siege. We will climb the cliff and drop boulders on the battlements."

"Possible perhaps, but very difficult."

"We will fire logs and thrust them into the passage; they shall blaze and smoulder, you will smoke and bake as the heat spreads. Do you defy the might of Lyonesse?"

The captain heaved a deep breath. "Of course not! As I declared from the very first, I gladly enter the service of the most gracious King Casmir! Ho, guards! Out for inspection!" (Suldrun's Garden; XII)

"... Unless you can prove a damage, you have suffered no loss."

"Legalisms! Sophistries! You have the sleight of words, by which poor peasants like me are mulcted and left helpless! Still, I would not have you think me a curmudgeon, and I hereby make you a gift of that fodder sequestered from my private reserve by your horse."

"I reject your gift!" declared Aillas. "Can you show articles from King Gax? If not, you can prove no title to the grass."

"I need prove nothing! Here on the second brake, the giving of a gift is certified by acceptance. Your horse, acting as your agent, accepted the gift, and you therefore become an extensionary donee."

At this moment the pack-horse raised high its tail and voided the contents of its gut. Aillas pointed to the pile of dung. "As you see, the horse tested your gift and rejected it. There is no more to be said."

"Fie! That is not the same grass!"

"It is near enough, and we cannot wait while you prove otherwise. Good-day, sir!" (The Green Pearl; XII, 2)

Spanchetta turned to Fleck. "I need not emphasize that Arles must receive a passing grade. Otherwise he will lose his Agency status."

Fleck shrugged. "He has much work to make up. The sooner he starts and the harder he works, the better his chances of passing."

"I will put this to him. Strangely, I dreamt of this entire episode last night. The dream began in just this fashion; I remember every word!"

"Amazing!" said Fleck. "Madame, I wish you good day."

Spanchetta paid no heed. "In the dream poor Arles was given a failing grade, which seemed to set in motion a whole string of misfortunes which even involved the instructor. It was a most realistic and rather terrible dream."

"I hope it is not precognition," said Fleck.

"Probably not. Still - who knows? Odd things happen."

Fleck considered a moment. "Your dream is the oddest of them all. As of this moment Arles is dropped from the class."
(Araminta Station; I, 6)

The Guild Delegate, the Sacerdote, the Immaculate, the Elderly Dame, the Hotel clerk – these are all key figures which oppose or interfere with our hero's quest. Bureaucracy rears its ugly head and bureaucrats are offended by the upsetting of their ordered worlds.

The Immaculate stepped forward. In plangent mock-Dirdir tones he spoke: "I will be expeditious; the ordinary ceremonies are inappropriate." He spoke to Reith, "Do you deny the charges?"

"I neither confirm nor deny them; they are ridiculous."

"It is my opinion that your statement is evasive. It signifies guilt. Additionally your attitudes are disrespectful. You are guilty." (The Dirdir; XX)

31

Glawen fetched the chair, emplaced it beside the desk. He seated himself after performing a small punctilious bow which he thought might mollify Miss Shoup but she spoke more crisply than ever: "I do not enjoy mockery, no matter how subliminal the level at which it is expressed."

"I am of the same opinion," said Glawen. "Unfortunately, it is pervasive and I ignore it as if it did not exist."

Miss Shoup raised her near-colorless eyebrows a hundredth of an inch, but made no comment. (Ecce and Old Earth; VII, 2)

The clerk creased his eyebrows in annoyance, then looked over his shoulder and brought the conversation to an end. He swung about and asked: "Well, sir? What are your needs?"

Glawen composed his voice. "Lodging, naturally."

"Unfortunately, sir, the hotel is complete. You must go elsewhere."

"What! The tourist office only just made my reservation!"

"Really?" The clerk shook his head. "Why am I not told of these things? They must have called elsewhere. Have you tried the Bon Felice?"

"Of course not. I was booked into the Novial; I came to the Novial. Does that sound unreasonable to you?"

"I am not the unreasonable one," said the clerk. "That word best describes the person who, when notified that no accommodation exists, continues to wheedle and argue. It is this conduct I define as unreasonable."

"Just so," said Glawen. "When the Tourist Information Office telephones down a booking, what is the procedure?"

"It is simple enough. The official on duty, which is to say, myself, carefully inscribes the name upon this board, and there is no scope for mistake."

Glawen pointed to the board. "What is the name in that blue square to the side?"

The clerk rose wearily to his feet. "This square? It reads: 'Glawen Clattuc.' So then?"

"I am Glawen Clattuc."

For a few seconds the clerk stood silent. Then he said: "You are lucky. That is our 'Grand Suite.' In the future you should take pains to explain your arrangements more carefully; we cannot function in the absence of facts." (Ecce and Old Earth; VII, 4)

"I am confused, certainly," said Maihac. "The leaps and bounds of your thinking have left me far behind, like a spotted hound chasing a coach through the dust."

Bariano smiled a cool smile. "If I am to correct you, I must speak without euphemism, but do not take offense!"

"Speak freely," said Maihac. "You might tell me something I don't know." (Night Lamp; XIII, 7)

32

Not all encounters are so civilized; sometimes the verbal sparring becomes more aggressive:

"You call us jackals?" demanded one of the Kash. "That is an insulting epithet!"

"Only for a creature who is not a jackal," said Karazan in a bored voice. (The Asutra; VI)

"By the way!" she said. "Mr. Maihac is bringing his silly froghorn. He may even try to play it, which should be great fun!"

"Ha hm," Hilyer growled. "So Maihac, among his other talents, is also a skilled musician!"

Althea laughed. "That remains to be seen. He won't prove it on the froghorn." (Night Lamp; III, 1)

The critics discuss Baron Bodissey's Life:
A monumental work if you like monuments...
...Pancreatic Review, St. Stephen, Boniface
Ponderously the great machine ingests its bales of lore; grinding, groaning, shuddering, it brings forth its product: small puffs of acrid vari-colored vapor.
...Excalibur, Patris, Krokinole
Six volumes of rhodomontade and piffle.
...Academia, London, Earth   (The Killing Machine; X)

"Vogel Filschner! I suppose it was not all his fault. His mother must have been a sloven. He had disgusting personal habits, such as picking his nose and examining the yield, making queer gulping noises, and above all smelling."   (The Palace of Love; IX)

Conversation between two Centennials of the Institute, in connection with third not present:
--I would gladly come to your house for a chat, if I did not suspect that Ramus were likewise invited."

--"But what is so wrong with Ramus? He often amuses me."

--"He is a fungus, a flatulence, a pompous old toad, and he irritates me vastly." (The Star King; VIII)

Carcolo said gruffly, "You sent me a message by old Alvonso."

Joaz nodded. "I trust he rendered my remarks accurately?"

Carcolo grinned wolfishly. "At times he felt obliged to paraphrase."

"Tactful old Alvonso."

"I am given to understand," said Carcolo, "that you consider me rash, ineffectual, callous to the best interests of Happy Valley. Alvonso admitted that you used the word 'blunderer' in reference to me."

Joaz smiled politely. "Sentiments of this sort are best transmitted through intermediaries." (The Dragon Masters; IV)

33

Even when insulting an opponent, the characters may do so in a passive-aggressive, indirect way:

... "Meanwhile, you may also pay your score as of this moment, in case you become suddenly indignant and prance off by night."
"That is a churlish remark to make to a gentleman!"
"No doubt. I am careful never to do so."   (The Green Pearl; IX, 6)

The short man now regarded Luke as he might an insect in his victual ration. "You talk like a Nonconformist. Excuse me if I seem offensive."
"Why apologize for something you can't help?" asked Luke and turned his back. (Dodkin's Job)

"Since your intellects are, in the main, of no great complexity, I will be terse." (Rhialto the Marvellous; XIV)

"I might point out that, over yonder, as smug as ever and no doubt as erroneous as ever in his theories, sits Clois Hutsenreiter. I worked with him once and even the laborers called him 'Careless Clois', and every night they would take away his money at some gambling game. Since then he has mended his fortunes, and has become Dean at an institution of higher learning. How did 'Careless Clois' achieve this office? By assiduous proctosculation, so I am told." (Night Lamp; XI, 2)

"It's very important that I speak with you; if you would be so good as to – "
"This importance exists from a single point of view." (The Palace of Love; V)

"One time I was bending to pick up a journal she had dropped and without so much as a by-your-leave here came the swish of the cane, catching me broad abeam. I was naturally disturbed and inquired why Her Ladyship had struck the blow. 'It was a matter of convenience,' she said. I started to say more but she waved her cane and told me to make a selection on the list of misdeeds for which I had gone unpunished and place a check-mark against the item." (Ecce and Old Earth; VI, 4)

And so the arguments eventually come to an end.

"Have you any further questions?"
"Bah," grumbled Kalash. "What good are questions when the answers are all non-sequiturs?" (Lurulu; II, 1)

34

Omon Bozhd spoke. "You really are irrational, Farr Sainh, if I may invest the word with its least offensive aura of meaning. (The Houses of Iszm; V)

...One day, at a garden party, a gentleman artlessly urged Dame Hester to write her memoirs. The fervor of her response caused him shock and dismay. "Ludicrous! Graceless! A beastly idea! How can I write memoirs now, when I have scarcely started to live?"

The gentleman bowed. "I see my mistake; it shall never be repeated!" (Ports of Call; I, 1)

"I am Captain Scharde Clattuc of Bureau B at Araminta Station. Please inform Titus Pompo that I want a few words with him on an official matter, at his earliest convenience; in fact now, if possible."

The clerk glanced at his colleagues; the three, after quick curious glances to gauge Scharde's seriousness, or, perhaps, sanity, returned to their work, disassociating themselves from so bizarre a problem. The clerk who had come forward spoke carefully: "Sir, I will see that your message is immediately disposed for the Oomphaw's attention."

A nuance in the clerk's phrasing caught Scharde's attention. "What does that mean?"

The clerk smilingly explained: "The message will be expedited to the Oomphaw's offices. No doubt an appropriate member of the staff will deliver to you, probably an application form upon which you may freely explain your needs."

"You don't quite understand," said Scharde. "I don't care for an application form; I want a few words with Titus Pompo, as soon as possible. Now would not be too soon."

The clerk's smile became strained. "Sir, let me use an open vocabulary. You do not seem an impractical visionary, with eyes raised to the glory of the ineffable. Still you apparently expect me to run to the Oomphaw's bedchamber, shake him awake and say: 'Up, sir, and out of bed quickly! A gentleman wants to talk with you.' I must inform you that this is not feasible." (Araminta Station; II, 9)

35

"Docking the boat"

Chapter Seven

In the summer of 1978 I married Liny. She was my girlfriend since we were both fourteen years old, so I can accurately say that we grew up together. We're still happily sharing our lives after all these years.

*She didn't read Science Fiction so, searching for appropriate romantic works I could share with her, I found the music of **The Carpenters** and **Bread** to be quite effective.*

During the preparation of this work I searched in Vance's books for quotes that I could share with my wife, perhaps a poem or other such sweet excerpt. Alas, Suldrun's doomed love, Zap 210's helplessnes or Keith Gersen's monomania did not fit the bill. The only excerpts I found interesting were humorous rather than romantic – and this may say more about me than about Vance!

Even so, I hope you will also enjoy the piquant, sometimes mordant humor present in the following passages:

Sexual costumes are most peculiar and complex, and cannot be analyzed here. The visitor, however, is earnestly warned never, under any circumstances, to make overtures to local women, since unpleasant consequences may be expected, the extreme penalty being marriage to the woman involved, or her mother.

--- from Handbook to the Planets and Gaean Cosmography (Ports of Call; II, 1)

"Lord Radkuth strained himself with a surfeit of lust, for our princesses are the most ravishing creations of human inspiration, just as I am the noblest of princes. But Lord Radkuth indulged himself too copiously, and thereby suffered a mortification. It is a lesson for us all." (The Eyes of the Overworld; I)

Sune nodded sagely. "I am told that the Eisel are an intemperate people, and that the girls lack all decorum. Do you wonder now at my caution? You will befriend some brassy creature with huge breasts and flaunting buttocks. I will be far from your mind while the creature instructs you in a dozen vulgar exercises." (Maske:Thaery; IX)

37

Melancthe sighed. "When you come back, you shall have all my love."

Shimrod reflected. "And we shall be lovers, in spirit and body: so you promise?"

Melancthe winced and closed her eyes. "Yes. I will praise you and caress you and you may commit your erotic fornications upon my body. Is that definite enough?"

"I will accept it in lieu of anything better." (Suldrun's Garden; XIV)

At puberty men wore blue-fringed headbands and girls red-fringed headbands; thereafter, they were oblivious to each other save as sexless blurs. Marriages were arranged and at the conclusion of the ceremony the bride and groom removed the colored fringes from each other's forehead, the presumption being that now, for the first time, they saw each other's faces, and perhaps in many cases it was so. The act had strong erotic symbolism, being tantamount to breaking the maidenhead. The excitement affected everyone present. At the raising of the fringes, bride and groom were required to feign gladsome surprise, then dance a traditional dance symbolic of initiation into the erotic mysteries. Everyone enjoyed the occasion, approving a proper performance of the dance, criticizing incorrect postures, reminiscing as to other dancings. (Ports of Call; XI)

So can we please have some useful advice about Love?

"You may know me as Cwyd. And you, sir, and your mistress?"

"I am Aillas, and this is Tatzel."

"She seems somewhat morose and out of sorts. Do you beat her often?"

"I must admit that I do not."

"There is the answer! Beat her well; beat her often! It will bring the roses to her cheeks! There is nothing better to induce good cheer in a woman than a fine constitutional beating, since they are exceptionally jolly during the intervals in an effort to postpone the next of the series."

A woman came to join them. "Cwyd speaks the truth! When he raises his fist to me I laugh and I smile, with all the good humour in the world, for my head is full of merry thoughts. Cwyd's beating has well served its purpose! Nevertheless Cwyd himself becomes gloomy, through bafflement. How did the roaches find their way into his pudding? Where except in Cwyd's small-clothes are household nettels known to grow? Sometimes as Cwyd dozes in the sunlight, a sheep wanders by and urinates in his face. Ghosts have even been known to skulk up behind Cwyd in the dark and beat him mercilessly with mallets and cudgels."

Cwyd nodded. "Admittedly, when Threlka is beaten for her faults, there is often a peculiar aftermath! Nonetheless, the basic concept is sound." (The Green Pearl; XII, 1)

Twisk spoke to Madouc: "I will remark, as a matter of casual interest, that Zocco is notorious for his lewd conduct. If you kissed his nose you would be compelled into his service, and soon would be kissing him elsewhere, at his orders, and who knows what else?"

"This is unthinkable!" declared Madouc aghast. "Zocco seemed so affable and courteous!"

"That is the usual trick." (Madouc; III, 3)

"Consider the consequences if everyone on Earth suddenly becomes clairvoyant and telepathic?"

"Chaos," muttered Tarbert, "Divorces by the hundreds." (The Brains of Earth; XI)

"At first glance she might seem mysterious and inscrutable. Why? Could it be that she is actually shy and demure, and emotionally immature?"

"Marvelous!" declared Glawen. "How do you divine all this, so quickly?

"I have had experience with these hoity-toity types," said Chilke modestly. "There is a trick for dealing with them."

"Hm," said Glawen. "Can you divulge a few details?"

"Of course! But keep in mind that patience is involved. You sit off by yourself, pretending disinterest, and watching the sky or a bird, as if your mind was fixed on something spiritual, and they can't stand it. Pretty soon they come walking past, twitching just a bit, and finally they ask your advice about something, or wonder if they can buy you a drink. After that, it is simply a matter of docking the boat."
(Throy; V, 7)

"An inkling of 'why'"

Chapter Eight

The beginning of my married life in Philadelphia coincided with the first of two important events that allowed me to significantly expand my Jack Vance library: DAW books started to publish his back catalogue.

*Although these books were sold everywhere, my favorite store was Hourglass Books in Center City, which sold only SF and Fantasy works; this was almost too good to be true! Here I found Gerrold and Niven's **The Flying Sorcerers** and James Hogan's first "Giants of Ganymede" story, **Inherit the Stars**.*

*And here I also bought **The Killing Machine** and **The Dirdir**. It would take me years to find the first book in the Demon Princes and Tschai series, but from that point on I wouldn't miss any other newly-published Vance book – ever!*

Favorite dictum of raffles, the amateur cracksman:
> **Money lost, little lost,**
> **Honor lost, much lost.**
> **Pluck lost, all lost.** (The Killing Machine; VIII)

With such abundant wordtools at his disposal, it is reasonable to expect Vance's characters to discourse on their life-beliefs.

> **Jubal turned to find the man with the three-tufted head-cloth again sitting in the bow of the scape. "I wish I knew how you do that," said Jubal.**
> **"You would gain nothing. Every instant a million events occur one iota past the edge of your awareness. Do you believe that?"**
> **"How can I dispute you?" Jubal answered sourly. "I know only what I can know. What I can't know, I don't know."**
> **"Do you wish to learn?"**
> **"Learn what?"**
> **"That is the wrong question. 'What' is constructed by each person for himself and in spite of himself. You can only learn 'how' and sometimes an inkling of 'why'."** (Maske:Thaery; XVII)

The heroes are usually pragmatic and sober - their philosophies concrete and rooted in reality. Sometimes they muse out loud on the nature of their existence:

Kirdy shook his head in bitter despair. "Why is it this? There are never answers to my questions. Why, indeed, am I alive?"

"Here, at least, the answer is self-evident," said Glawen. "You are alive because you are not dead."

Kirdy darted Glawen a suspicious glance. "Your remark is more subtle than perhaps you intended it to be. For a fact I cannot conceive of any other condition, which may well be a compelling argument in favor of immortality."

"Possibly so," said Glawen. "I, personally, find it easy to conceive of this other condition. I can readily imagine myself alive and you dead. Does this weaken your argument in favor of immortality?"

"You have missed the whole point," said Kirdy. (Araminta Station; VII, 5)

"Have you visited other worlds?

"Dozens. I was born beside a star so far that you'll never see its light, not in the sky of Halma."

"Then why are you here?

"I often ask myself the same. The answer always comes: because I'm not somewhere else. Which is a statement more sensible than it sounds. And isn't it a marvel? Here am I and here are you; think of it! When you ponder the breadth of the galaxy, you must recognize a coincidence of great singularity!

"I don't understand."

"Simple enough! Suppose you were here and I elsewhere, or I were here and you elsewhere, or both of us were elsewhere; three cases vastly more probable than the fourth, which is the fact of our mutual presence within ten feet of each other. I repeat, a miraculous concatenation! And to think that some hold the Age of Wonders to be past and gone!" (Emphyrio; II)

Roger, wandering through the saloon, picked up a book and read a trifle of speculation from the pen of the eminent cosmologist Dennis Kertesz: "Infinity is a fascinating idea with which all of us have struggled. Especially the infinity of extension, which cannot be evaded by proposing a universe of finite circumference. Less carefully considered is an infinity in the other direction: the infinity of smallness, and it extends as far and is as bemusing as that other infinity.

"What happens to matter at the lower reaches? Matter exhibits a constantly finer texture, until it no longer can be dealt with experimentally, or even mathematically. Eventually, or so it would seem, all matter, all energy, all everything, even space itself, must be expressed by some single antithesis: a basic yes or no; back or forth; in or out; clock-wise or counter-clock-wise; fourth-dimensional coiling in, or fourth-dimensional coiling out. Even at this level, the infinite recession into smallness continues. No matter how small is anything it serves only as a gauge by which to define extremes (if only formal extremes) a hundred times smaller..."

Roger, already suffering melancholy, found the cosmic immensities appalling, and laid aside the book. (Space Opera; VII)

Often philosophy is expostulated from a jaundiced point of view:

"These are interesting concepts," said Schwatzendale. "But for myself, I do not care to grope among such tenuous ideas. I deal only with what is here and now. Everything else is foam and mist."

"Yours is a simple methodology," said the tanner politely. "Perhaps, ultimately, it is the wisest way of all, since the theorist is forced to wrestle with a dozen possibilities, each making its special pleading."

Schwatzendale laughed. "I have not theorized even to this effect! I celebrate the concrete! If I locate an itch, I scratch it! If I discover a leek and mutton pie, I eat it. If I come upon a beautiful woman, I make myself agreeable. (Ports of Call; V, 3)

Hilario indignantly pointed out these deficiencies to Shylick and demanded that the work be done properly, to exact standards. Shylick, now glum and out of sorts, did his best to evade the extra toil. He argued that total precision was impossible and unknown to the cosmos. He claimed that a reasonable and realistic person accepted a degree of latitude in the interpretation of his contract, since this looseness was inherent in the communicative process.

Hilario remained inflexible and Shylick became ever more excited, striking at the floor with his tall green hat, and his arguments ever more abstruse. He stated that since the distinction between 'seeming' and 'substance' was in any case no more than a philosophical nicety, almost anything was equivalent to almost anything else. Hilario said gravely: "In that case, I will pay off my account with this bit of straw." (Madouc; VII, 1)

Shimrod sauntered forward. "Why must you beat poor Grofinet?"

"Why does one do anything?" growled the troll. "From a sense of purpose. For the sake of a job well done!"

"That is a good response, but it leaves many questions unanswered," said Shimrod. (Suldrun's Garden; XIII)

"If you are you – if you are an "I", an individual – the cosmos is thrown into turmoil. You'd have the distinction of challenging an entire universe – merely by existing. Do you exist?"

"You poured out two jolts of that Scotch. You drank one, I drank the other. They're both gone. I guess that answers your question." (The House on Lily Street; X)

Here are philosophic discourses about money, and the toil required to obtain it:

"Willingly will I aid you," said Pandelume. "There is, however, another aspect involved. The universe is methodized by symmetry and balance; in every aspect of existence is this equipoise observed. Consequently, even in the trivial scope of our dealings, this equivalence must be maintained, thus and thus. I agree to assist you; in return, you perform a service of equal value for me. When you have completed this small work, I will instruct and guide you to your complete satisfaction." (The Dying Earth: Turjan of Miir)

Shugart said: "Money has always been our great problem, even though the philosophy is simple."
"I wish I found it so," said Kiper wistfully.
"Nothing to it," said Shugart. "First, locate someone with money. Second, learn what he wants more than the money. Third, make this available to him. It works every time." (Araminta Station; IV, 3)

"Poverty is acceptable because then there is no way but up. Rich people worry about losing their wealth, but I like this worry far more than the worry of scratching the wealth together in the first place. Also, people are nicer to you when they think you are rich - although they'll often hit you over the head to find out where you hide your money." (Araminta Station; I, 4)

For a moment Esteban stood speechless. Then, half-laughing, he said: "But Jantiff, dear naïve Jantiff! I don't want to augment my capabilities! This implies a predisposition for work. For civilized men work is an unnatural occupation!"
"I suppose there is no inherent virtue in work," Jantiff conceded. "Unless, of course, it is performed by someone else." (Wyst: Alastor 1716; IV)

"Property and life are not incommensurable, when property is measured in human toil. Essentially property is life; it is that proportion of life which an individual has expended to gain the property. When a thief steals property, he steals life. Each act of pillage therefore becomes a small murder." (The Anome, VI)

And yet, not all is irony or sarcasm. As we read his pages, Vance can present us with some rather interesting soul-searches worthy of deeper consideration:

"Young folk often want change simply for the sake of change, that they may bring significance and identity to their own lives. It is an ultimate form of narcissism." (Ecce and Old Earth; III, 1)

44

If the study of human interactions could become a science, I suspect that an inviolate axiom might be discovered to this effect: Every social disposition creates a disparity of advantages. Further: Every innovation designed to correct the disparities, no matter how altruistic in concept, works only to create a new and different set of disparities. (The Brave Free Men; VI)

"...Living creatures, if nothing else, have the right to life. It is their only truly precious possession, and the stealing of life is a wicked theft..." (The Dying Earth: T'sais)

"Whatever is, is! Whatever is, is right! Whatever is right, is good! Whatever is good has existence, and therefore 'is'; and the Circle is whole." (Ports of Call; IV, 4)

A surfeit of honey cloys the tongue; a surfeit of wine addles the brain; so a surfeit of ease guts a man of strength. (The Dying Earth: Ulan Dhor)

What is an evil man? The man is evil who coerces obedience to his private ends, destroys beauty, produces pain, extinguishes life. (Star King; II)

Like most, if not all, games, hussade is symbolic war. (Wyst: Alastor 1716; Glossary 4)

The mind was a marvelous instrument, thought Shimrod; when left to wander untended, it often arrived at curious destinations. (Madouc; XI, 2)

"The past is never real," said Nai the Hever. "The flux of events is the present; unless you are able to enforce a pattern upon this flux, it is wiser not to try" (Maske: Thaery, XIII)

These next two passages could be subjects of debate in any philosophy course:

"In a situation of infinity, every possibility, no matter how remote, must find physical expression."
"Does that mean yes or no?"
"Both and neither." (Emphyrio; VII)

The young man cried out, raising his voice to be heard against the wind: "But is it good news or bad?"
"It is neither," said Egon Tamm. "It is reality."
"Ah!" came the disconsolate cry. "That may be the worst of all!" (Throy; I, 2)

I think it is fitting to close off this chapter on philosophical discussions with perhaps the ultimate question: What is Truth?

" 'Truth'?" Cuireg made an indolent gesture. " 'Truth' is a refuge for weak minds – why concern yourself? It is a non-functional notion, like the square root of negative infinity or, if you prefer, a mare's nest. The good Baron Bodissey issued a definitive dictum: 'Truth is a barnacle on the arse of progress.'" (Lurulu; XI, 4)

" 'Truth' is contained in the preconceptions of him who seeks to define it." (The Languages of Pao; XI)

Myron, who had been following the conversation, ventured a comment. "I am told that Unspiek Baron Bodissey was once called upon to define truth. His views are not exactly relevant, but, as always, they are illuminating."

"Don't stop now," said Schwatzendale, who also had been listening. "On with the anecdote!"

"It goes like this. One dark midnight a student entered the Baron's chamber and awoke the Baron from his sleep. The student cried out, 'Sir, I am distraught with anxiety! Tell me once and for all: what is Truth?'

"The Baron groaned and cursed and finally raised his head. He roared, 'Why do you bother me with such trivia?'

"The student gave a faltering response. 'Because I am ignorant and you are wise!'

"Very well, then! I can reveal to you that Truth is a rope with one end!'

"The student persisted. 'All very well, sir! But what of the far end which is never found?'

"'Idiot!' stormed the Baron. 'That is the end to which I refer!' And the Baron once more composed himself to sleep."
(Ports of Call; X, 2)

"The quiet area"

Chapter Nine

Liny and I continued our studies in Philadelphia through the early 80s. Finances were fairly tight, which is why I usually roamed the used bookstore shelves looking for SF books to read.

*Dubois Bookshop on Sansom St. and The Book Swap on Ridge Avenue were common haunts, where I bought books like Robert L. Forward's **Dragon's Egg** as well as Spider Robinson's **Callahan's Crosstime Saloon**. These used bookstores were very important to me, not only because I could get these titles at a significant discount, but also because they were often the only place where I might find a book that had run out*

its print.

*I became obsessed with seeking out these used bookstores; everywhere I traveled I was on the lookout for them. It was during an interview for Ophthalmology residency that I found the first Demon Prince book, **The Star King**, at The Book Rack in North Olmsted, Ohio. During another interview trip, Oh Joy! I found both **City of the Chasch** and **The Anome** at Books and Art in Gretna, VA.*

*And so my Jack Vance collection began to grow by leaps and bounds with used copies of the DAW editions: **Nopalgarth**, **Trullion**, **The Blue World** and **Big Planet** soon followed. By now I began to realize that Jack Vance meant a lot more to me than I had suspected. After all, why get so excited about finding a dusty used copy of **Magnus Ridolph**?*

And surely because of our financial situation, with more studying in the future and our first child on the way, I began to observe how often money became a theme in these books. Whether fighting over fortunes, or squabbling over mere Zinks, the bargaining characters in these passages cover the entire breadth of Vance's book-writing career.

"What happened to the documents?"

"They left my hands long ago."

"Do you know where they are now?"

Keebles shook his head. "I know to whom I sold them. What happened next I can't even guess."

"Is it possible the buyer still has them in his possession?"

"Anything is possible."

"Well then: to whom did you sell them?"

Keebles, leaning back, put his feet on the desk. "We are now moving into the quiet area, where words are golden. This is where we take off our shoes and go on tiptoe."

"I've played such games before," said Glawen. "Someone has always stolen my shoes." (Ecce and Old Earth; VIII, 4)

The struggle over remuneration appears very early in Vance's works:

Paddy said, "We need a special ultraviolet light source for our camera. It must have four separate units with variable frequency controls for each unit over the range six hundred to three thousand one hundred angstroms. Can you make it up?"

Dane scratched his pate. "I'll see if I've got the proper valves. I think I can do it." He cocked a bright glance at Fay. "It'll cost you dear, though. Three hundred marks."

Paddy drew back in indignation. "Faith, now. I'll use my flashlight first. Three hundred marks for a few bits of wire and junk?"

"There's my labor, lad, and my training. Long years now I've studied."

Two hundred fifty marks was the figure finally reached, delivery to be made in two days. (The Five Gold Bands; X)

Honoraries are often a source of discussion. "Human toil", we have been told, is the most basic unit of monetary value. Thus, services must be paid for:

He spoke in a voice of great dignity. "As a practical man I can't operate on speculation. I would require a retaining fee of ten thousand sequins." He blew out his cheeks and glanced toward Reith. "Upon receipt of this sum, I would immediately exert my influence to set your scheme into motion."

"All very well," said Reith. "But, as a ridiculous supposition, let us assume that, rather than a man of honor, you were a scoundrel, a knave, a cheat. You might take my money, then find the project impossible for one reason or another, and I would have no recourse. Hence I can pay only for actual work accomplished." (The Dirdir; XII)

"Well then, how much money do you offer?"

"My plans have not progressed to that stage. What do you consider a suitable fee?"

"To risk life and freedom? I would not stir for less than fifty thousand sequins."

Reith rose to his feet. "You have your fifty sequins; I have my information. I trust you to keep my secret."

Zarfo sat sprawled back in his chair. "Now then, not so fast. After all I am old and my life is not worth so much after all. Thirty thousand? Twenty? Ten?"

"The figure starts to become practical." (Servants of the Wankh; VII)

Fariske attempted the cogency of pure logic. "What, after all. is the fetching of a few percebs? The day contains only so many minutes; it passes as well one way as another."

"In that case, go fetch them yourself!" (Wyst: Alastor 1716; XII)

Still, there's always someone trying to get something for nothing...

"Further," said Maloof, "we want to cruise the river for a few hours tomorrow. For preference we will use the Lulio. I expect that this is a service that you offer to guests at the inn without charge?"

"Wrong! We rent the Lulio out at a rate of seven sols per day."

Maloof raised his eyebrows in shock. "That is a large sum! We can swim the river free of charge."

"True, and you will lose your private parts to the glass-fish within the minute. Swimming is a poor economy."

In the end Maloof secured the Lulio for five sols, payment to be made in advance. (Lurulu; V, 5)

"I am conducting an official survey," said Julian coldly. "I need and I expect both convenience and flexibility."

Chilke gave a good-humored chuckle. "Think just a bit. This flyer is here and ready to go, which is true convenience. It takes you wherever you point it, also up and down. That is flexibility. How much are you paying?"

"Nothing whatever, naturally."

"There's your flyer. You can't do better anywhere for the price." (Araminta Station; V, 3)

Oswig stopped short, as if at a sudden recollection. "Now it occurs to me! The warehousemen are not on duty – they have gone off to games at the Ballingay Traces. But there should be no real inconvenience; I expect that your crew will discharge the cargo for us, as a courtesy."

"Certainly," said Maloof. "We have done such work before, and we can do it again. Our fee will be the standard fifty sols."

Oswig cried out in shock. "Do my ears hear correctly? Did you truly mention the sum 'fifty sols'? Have you no morality whatever? How can a gentleman swindle with such aplomb?"

Maloof held up his hand. "I will answer your questions in the order they were asked. Yes, your ears are functioning properly. Yes, the price quoted was fifty sols. Yes, I use the morality of the working spaceman, which is compact but versatile. And I can explain the basis of our rates: often an official begs for a free service, as a courtesy, then puts the savings into his own pocket. Our schedule of fees is intended to curb this nuisance." (Lurulu; VII, 1)

Contracts, therefore, are of utmost importance:

Cugel attempted an apologetic smile. "I never take without giving in return. This policy averts misunderstandings."

Iucounu's eyelids drooped at at the corners in moist reproach. "Must we quibble over minor points? Into the carriage with you, Cugel; you may enlarge upon your qualms as we ride."

"Very well," said Cugel. "I will ride with you to Taun Tassel, but you must accept these three terces in full, exact, final, comprehensive and complete compensation for the ride and every other aspect, adjunct, by-product and consequence, either direct or indirect, of the said ride, renouncing every other claim, now, and forever, including all times of the past and future, without exception, and absolving me, in part and in whole, from any and all further obligations."

Iucounu held up small balled fists and gritted his teeth toward the sky. (Cugel's Saga; VI, 2)

Inch by inch, foot by foot, the hole sank into the old seabed, but not at a rate to suit Rhialto. At last he complained to Um-Foad: "What is wrong with the work-force? They saunter here and there; they laugh and gossip at the water-barrel; they stare into space for long periods. That old gaffer yonder, he moves so seldom that twice I hace feared for his life."

Um-Foad made an easy response: "Come now, Rhialto! Do not forever be carping and chiding! These men are being paid handsomely by the hour. They are in no hurry to see the end of so noble an enterprise. As for the old man, he is my uncle Yaa-Yimpe, who suffers severe back pains, and is also deaf. Must he be penalized on this account? Let him enjoy the same perquisite as the others!"

Rhialto shrugged. "As you wish. Our contract encompasses situations of this sort."

"Eh? How so?"

"Refer to the section: 'Rhialto at his option may pay all charges on the basis of cubic footage removed from the hole. The amount of said payment shall be determined by the speed at which Rhiato, standing beside a pile of soft dirt with a stout shovel, can transfer ten cubic feet of said dirt to a new pile immediately adjacent.'"

Um-Foad cried out in consternation, and consulted the contract. "I do not remember including any such provision!"

"I added it as an afterthought," said Rhialto. "Perhaps you failed to notice."

Um-Foad darted away to exhort the workers. Grudgingly they bent to their shovels, and even old Yaa-Yimpe shifted his position from time to time. (Rhialto the Marvellous; XV)

Examine these passages, where lodging accommodations are squabbled over:

"Our business here is ordinary: we seek food and shelter during this stormy night for which we will pay in suitable degree."

"I can provide shelter," said the crofter. "As for payment, 'suitable' for me might be 'unsuitable' for you. Sometimes these misunderstandings put folk at the outs."

Aillas searched the contents of his wallet. "Here is a silver half-florin. If this will suffice, we have eliminated the problem." (The Green Pearl; XII, 1)

"Can you direct me to an inexpensive hotel of good quality?"

"The official rubbed his chin. "Your requirements contradict each other..." (Ports of Call; III, 1)

"I cannot in good conscience recommend the Mirlview. Persons of judgement and high connections inevitably select the Rolinda. True, it is expensive, but what of that? If disbursing a dinket or two causes a person pain, he should best stay home, where his frugalities will not offend members of the travel industry." (Araminta Station; VII, 2)

Glawen alighted, removed his luggage from the bin while Maxen sat drumming his fingers on the wheel. Glawen paid the standard fee, which Maxen accepted with raised eyebrows. "And the gratuity?"

Glawen slowly turned to stare into the driver's compartment. "Did you help me load my luggage?"

"No, but - "

"Did you help me unload it?"

"By the same token - "

"Did you not tell me that I was inbred and eccentric, and probably weak-minded?"

"That was a joke."

"Now can you guess the location of you gratuity?"

"Yes. Nowhere." (Araminta Station; IX, 1)

Food must of course be consumed, but at what price?

He signaled to the woman. "Madame, our account, if you please."

The woman looked over the platters. "You have eaten ravenously. I will need two or, better, three SVU from each of you."

Rackrose cried out in protest. "Three SVU for a few mouthfuls of food? That would be exorbitant at the Domus!"

"The Domus serves insipid gulch. Pay your account or I will sit on your head."

...Gersen handed over the coins and Madame Tintle departed.

Rackrose gave a snort of disgust. "You are far too obliging. The woman's avarice is matched only by the vileness of her cuisine."

Madame Tintle spoke over his shoulder. "By chance I overheard that remark. On your next visit I will boil up my crotch-strap for your chatowsies." (The Face; III)

Jantiff finished his meal and the attendant gave him a slip of paper. "Please pay at the main desk."

Jantiff glanced at the slip in wonder. "Two ozols. Can this price be correct?"

"The price may not be 'correct,'" said the attendant. "Still it's the price we exact here at the Traveler's Inn." (Wyst: Alastor 1716; III)

What about transportation?

"What would be the price for a decent vessel?"

"Five thousand toldecks, or more."

"At seventeen toldecks a week? This is a long-range goal."

"Somehow you must augment your income."

"Easier said than done."

"Not at all. The secret is to seize upon the opportunity and wring it dry."

"No such opportunity has ever been offered to me."

"That is the common complaint." (Maske: Thaery; VI)

"Ten terces is the value of a new wheel," said the oldest brother. "Pay over that sum at once. Since I never threaten I will not mention the alternatives."

Cugel drew himself up. "I am not one to be impressed by bluster!"

"What of cudgels and pitchforks?" (Cugel's Saga; III, 2)

Wayness alighted from the cab. "I see that you are something of a philosopher."

"True! It is in my blood! But first and foremost, I am a Cossack!"

"And what is a Cossack?"

The driver stared incredulously. "Can I believe my ears? But now I see that you are an off-worlder. Well then, a Cossack is a natural aristocrat; he is fearless and steadfast, and cannot be coerced. Even as a cab driver he conducts himself with Cossack dignity. At the end of a journey, he does not calculate his fare; he announces the first figure that comes into his head. If the passenger does not choose to pay, well then: what of that? The driver gives him a single glance of contempt and drives off in disdain."

"Interesting. And what fare are you calling out to me?"

"Three sols."

"That is far too much. Here is a sol. You may accept it or drive off in disdain." (Ecce and Old Earth; V, 3)

Even rest & relaxation is not immune from bargaining. For example, going to the Pussycat Palace, a house of prostitution...

A few minutes later Fader appeared. "Is everyone on hand?"

52

Shugart said: "Two of the group aren't up to it. There'll be just seven."

"I still must charge nine sols, since that was the quoted price, and I turned down another job in order to keep faith with you."

"Seven persons: seven sols, gratuity included. That is all you will get from us," said Shugart. "Take it or leave it."

Fader shook his bronze curls in pain. "You Araminta workers are both hard and crooked; I pity the poor girls at the Palace if your erections are of similar quality." (Araminta Station; IV, 7)

Finally there is shopping: the ultimate test of a consummate bargainer. Learn from these masterful examples, as characters haggle over cusps, a stone effigy, and – don't be fooled! - a pair of candelabra.

"Such a cusp of violet glass I value at a hundred terces," replied the glass-blower in a casual manner.

"What?" cried Cugel in outrage. "Do I appear so gullible? The charge is excessive."

The glass-blower replaced his tools, swages and crucibles, showing no concern for Cugel's indignation. "The universe evinces no true stability. All fluctuates, cycles, ebbs and flows; all is pervaded with mutability. My fees, which are immanent with the cosmos, obey the same laws and vary according to the anxiety of the costumer."

... Taking the cusps, Cugel tossed three terces to the worktable. "All is mutability, and thus your hundred terces has fluctuated to three." (The Eyes of the Overworld; VII)

"That is a fine piece - very rare, very valuable! I make you a good price, because I like you!"

"How can it be rare?" demanded Dame Hester. "I took it from this tray where there are thirty more just like it!"

"You do not see with the eyes of a connoisseur! That is an image of the Garre Mountain effrit, who casts thunder-stones. This piece is especially lucky and will win your gambles at the dogfights! Since I am poor and ignorant, I will let you have it for the laughable price of twenty sols!"

Dame Hester stared at her in angry amazement. "It is true that I am laughing! Clearly you lack all decency to ask any price whatever for this repulsive little geegaw! Do you take me for a fool? I am seriously insulted."

"No matter. I insult better folk than you several times a day. It is no novelty; in fact, it is a pleasure."

Dame Hester brought out a coin. "This is the value I place upon that horrid little item, and only for the pleasure it will give me when I describe your miserable shop to my friends."

"Bah," said the woman. "Take it at no charge. You shall never gloat that you outdid me in noblesse oblige. Take it and be gone!"

"Why not? I shall do so. Please wrap it for me tastefully."

"I am too busy." (Ports of Call; II, 2)

While they waited, Althea had gone to rummage through a ramshackle old shop, where oddments of this and that were offered for sale. In a casual pile she noted a pair of massive copper candelabra, from which she hastily averted her eyes and went to examine what seemed to be a dented old pot. "A valuable piece," the shopkeeper told her. "That is genuine aluminum."

"I'm not really interested," said Althea. "I already have a pot."

"Just so. Perhaps you like those old candle-holders? Very valuable: pure copper!"

"I don't think so," said Althea. "I already have a pair of candelabra, as well."

"Very handy if one of them broke," argued the shopkeeper. "It is not good to be without light."

"True," said Althea. "What do you want for the dirty old things?"

"Not much. About five hundred sols."

Althea merely turned him a scornful look, and went to study a stone plaque, highly polished and intricately carved with glyphs. "What is this thing?"

"It is very old. I can't read it. They say it tells the ten human secrets: very important, I should think."

"Not unless you can read this odd script."

"Better than nothing."

"How much?"

"Two hundred sols."

"Surely you're joking!" cried Althea indignantly. "Do you take me for a fool?"

"Well seventy sols then. A great bargain: seven sols per secret!"

"Bah. Those secrets are old and useless, even if I could read them. My price is five sols."

"Aiee! Must I give valuables to every crazy woman that walks into the shop?" Althea haggled long and devoutly, but the shopkeeper held to a price of forty sols.

"The price is reprehensible!" stormed Althea. "I'll pay it only if you include some extra pieces of lesser value: let us say, this rug and, well, why not? those candelabra."

Again the shopkeeper showed distress. He patted the rug, which was woven in stripes of black, russet and russet-gold. "This is a fecundity rug. It is woven from the pubic hairs of virgins! The candlesticks are six thousand years old, from the cave of the first Hermit King Jon Solander. I value the three items at a thousand sols!"

"I will pay forty for all."

The shopkeeper handed Althea a scimitar and bared his throat. "Kill me first before you dishonor me with such robbery!"

In the end, somewhat dazed, Althea walked from the shop, carrying candelabra, plaque and rug... (Night Lamp; III, 1)

"Change utterly!"

Chapter Ten

The mid-80s were the years of my final medical training. We moved to Durham, North Carolina for my ophthalmology training at Duke University. Those years saw the birth of our sons, Rick and Javi, and a serious lack of free time to read non-medical books.

Still, I often traveled over to the nearby town of Chapel Hill to a wonderful used bookstore on Franklin St. Here I bought copies of Gregory Benford's Artifact and Gaiman & Pratchett's Good Omens. Durham had another used bookstore on North Gregson St., and it was here that I bought the paperback edition of The Asutra, replacing the F&SF magazines I had saved so long before.

These were also the years when Jack Vance returned to his Dying Earth, publishing both Cugel's Saga and Rhialto the Marvellous. Any new Jack Vance book was an exciting event, and I wouldn't wait to pick up a used copy; I bought them new as soon as they hit the bookstores.

Then something extraordinary happened: Vance published the Lyonesse trilogy, not related to any of his previous works. It would become (in many critics' opinion) his Fantasy masterpiece!

**DR FIDELIUS
THAUMATURGE, PAN-SOPHIST, MOUNTEBANK**

Relief for Cankers, Gripes and Spasms

**SPECIAL TREATMENT OF SORE KNEES
Expert Advice: Free**
(Suldrun's Garden; XXV*)*

Expert advice – for free? There is, indeed, much wisdom to be gleaned from these stories (underlining is by me).

"Over a lifetime I've learned a hundred little tricks which I call lubrications. Most of them I keep to myself, but I'll share one of them with you, free of charge; 'Never push too hard at anything, it might start pushing back.'" (Araminta Station; I, 5)

55

"I wonder, sir, if you'd be good enough to advise me."

"Certainly, within the limits of discretion," said Eubanq. "I should warn you, however, that free advice is usually not worth its cost." (Wyst: Alastor 1716; XII)

Considering that we've paid money for these books, however, then we aren't really seeking "free advice". We therefore peruse them for their pearls of knowledge and guidance.

Problems are like the trees of Bleadstone Woods; there is always a way between. (The Book of Dreams; XIV)

"What is it again that I am supposed to learn?"

"Remain honest, steadfast and true! Adopt no weird philosophies. Avoid exotic cults and intellectual miasma."

"You should have told me sooner," said Sunje. "The hay is in the barn." (Throy; IX, 3)

"I suggest also that you say nothing unless you are directly addressed, and then reply with a platitude. Before long everyone will think you a brilliant conversationist." (Araminta Station; I, 3)

"When opportunity comes fleeting past, seize it by the heels before it seizes you!" --- mad poet Narvath ---   (Ports of Call; VIII, 2)

"It is always reckless to challenge powerful men, unless you can bring to bear a compensating power." (Maske:Thaery; XIII)

"A person who conceals his curiosity has knowledge thrust upon him, so I have learned." (The Brave Free Men; XIV)

Some of the sayings we encounter sound like they should *be part of our popular culture:*

Chilke surveyed the room with care. "Never did I think I would set foot in Poolie's again. A philosopher, whose name eludes me, once declared: 'Life is incredible unless you are alive.'* (Throy; V, 3)

... there was an ancient aphorism to the effect that eavesdroppers hear no good of themselves. (Son of the Tree; V)

One thing was certain: when someone searched into secret places, he often came up with things he would rather not have found. (Night Lamp; V, 3).

"There may be something in what you say. But remember -" he held high a pink forefinger "- <u>no dogma fits every dog!</u>" (Ports of Call; IV, 3)

"As of now: you find her unappealing?"

Glawen wondered how best to phrase his remarks. "Spacemen encounter all kinds of women. I have heard them say that <u>at night all cats are gray.</u>" (Araminta Station; VII, 3)

"You must use a bit of flirtation – not to excess, mind you! Let him know that you understand what he has in mind. <u>Mischief in a girl is like salt on meat...</u>" (Suldrun's Garden, VII)

'If you start a fight with your hands in your pockets, you'll have warm hands but a bloody nose!' (The Blue World; II)

Whether or not we understand some of this advice seems secondary to the sheer joy of reading it:

From the Teaching of Didram Bodo Sime, 6:6
   (Obloquies against the Toper and his Drink)
   Motto:
      It is not good to inebriate nor to souse, using swillage, near of far beers, or distillations.
   Expansion:
      The Toper is a fuming bore, a loon, a mongrel, a social mockery. Often he soils his clothes and commits malditties. He smells and belches; his familiarities trouble all decent folk. His songs and tirrilays offend the ears. He often gives breath to scurrilous conjecture. (The Book of Dreams; XII)

"We've been discussing Fanscherade."

"How very nice!" said Marucha. "Have you brought him around?"

"I hardly think so," said Akadie with a grin. "<u>The seed must lie before it germinates.</u>" (Trullion: Alastor 2262; V)

"Never try to cheat an honest man," said Etzwane. "Another thief might sympathize with your goals." (The Asutra; XI)

Bustamonte held up his hand. "Not so fast. <u>Today is not yesterday.</u>" (The Languages of Pao; III)

Sometimes the advice is neither given nor received – or, at least, not appreciated!

In many cases, believing that each condition generates its own counter-condition, he stands aloof, fearing to introduce a confusing

57

third factor. <u>When in doubt, do nothing</u>: this is one of the Connatic's favorite credos. (Marune: Alastor 2262; prologue)

Akadie had only just arisen from his bed. His hair was rumpled into wisps; his eyes were barely half-open. Nevertheless he gave Glinnes an affable good-morning. "Please <u>do not expound your business before breakfast; the world is not yet in focus</u>." (Trullion: Alastor 2262; IX)

Casmir, faintly frowning, stood with feet apart and hands behind his back. He disliked opposition to his judgments, especially from a girl so small and inexperienced. In a measured voice intended to define the facts with exactitude and finality he said: "<u>Your preference must on occasion yield to the forces of reality</u>." (Suldrun's garden; III)

Here are some of my very favorite ones:

Dame Maugelin returned to the room, panting in haste and excitement. "Your father commands you to the banquet. He wishes you to be everything a beautiful princess of Lyonesse should be. Do you hear? You may wear your blue velvet gown and your moonstones. At all times remember court etiquette! Don't spill your food; drink very little wine. Speak only when you are addressed, then respond with courtesy and without chewing your words. Neither titter, nor scratch yourself, nor wriggle in your chair as if your bottom itched. Do not belch, gurgle or gulp. If someone breaks wind, do not stare or point or attempt to place the blame. Naturally you will control yourself as well; <u>nothing is more conspicuous than a farting princess</u>. Come! I must brush your hair." (Suldrun's Garden; III)

"She'll be sorely vexed to see us going off to the tavern, and I'll eat slops for a week. Still, let's be away. <u>A man must never heed the woman's roar</u>." (The Face; V)

"The wine is of prime quality, as I specified; you need not fear agues nor gripes. Still, moderation, I beg of all of you!"
"But not too much of it!" Dobbo called out. "We'd be defeating only ourselves. <u>Moderation must be practiced in moderation</u>." (Wyst: Alastor 1716; VII)

Do not expectorate at random. Do not inappropriately void bowels or bladder; use designated receptacles. Do not perform an indiscreet flatulence except in designated areas. Make no loud, unpleasant or unreasonable noises; play no offensive music from a mechanical device; display no prurient images. (Ports of Call; III, 1)

"I merely suggested a possibility."
"<u>The inconceivable, sir, is rarely possible</u>." (The Book of Dreams; III)

Every birthday these become more relevant to me:

The aircar rose at a stomach-gripping rate, and from the engine box came a stuttering wheeze which caused Efraim to twist about in alarm. "Is this vehicle finally disintegrating?"

Flaussig listened with a puzzled frown. "A mysterious sound certainly, one which I have not heard before. Still, were you as old as this vehicle, your viscera would also produce odd noises. <u>Let us be tolerant of the aged.</u>" (Marune: Alastor 933; VI)

Gassoon jerked at the lapels of his coat. "I am not after all so old."

"Of course not. <u>A man is only old when he abandons his dreams.</u>" (Showboat World, VII)

Unspiek must of course be listened to:

"Honest folk do not wear masks when they enter a bank." - Baron Bodissey   (Night Lamp; III, 1)

"Only losers cry out for fair play." - Baron Bodissey in his philosophical encyclopedia of twelve volumes entitled LIFE (Night Lamp; II, 2)

Some characters can even advise us from beyond the grave:

"Do not be fooled: <u>we are all mortal, as I now attest.</u>" Excerpt from Rolf Marr Gersen's will.   (The Star King; II)

"Goodbye, or so I fear, Eustace. <u>I am not afraid of death; I just don't think I will like it very much.</u>" excerpt from Floyd Swaner's will, (Ecce and Old Earth; X, 2)

Finally here's the most devastating piece of advice ever given!

"I will give you advice, if you agree to act by it."
"At least I will listen."
"<u>Change utterly.</u>" (Suldrun's Garden; XXVI)

"I shall refrain from thinking"

Chapter Eleven

Once I finished my medical training it was then time to decide where to settle down. We moved to the greater Orlando area in Florida to start my private practice, specializing in the transplants of ocular tissues. Like the Optidynes of Mercantil, a corneal transplant can restore a person's sight otherwise lost to trauma or disease.

My daughter Monica was born the same year that saw the completion of the Lyonesse story. She's definitely more Madouc than Suldrun, I'm glad to say!

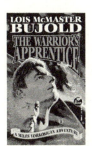

In the 90s I continued to discover exciting new authors, and thoroughly enjoyed Lois McMaster Bujold's **Vorkosigan** *books, C.F. Friedman's* **Cold Fire** *trilogy and the fiction of Connie Willis.*

The only World Science Fiction Convention I've attended was 1992's Magicon, held in Orlando. To my delight, Jack Vance was the guest of honor and I had a chance to meet him as he signed a copy of **The Jack Vance Lexicon**✸.

As I was excitedly waiting in line for his autograph, I kept practicing what I would say to him. He looked just like the pictures I'd seen, with a gentle, amused smile on his lips. You might imagine, therefore, my distress when I realized he had vision problems and could no longer read well! It may be irrational but, as an eye physician, I felt personally affronted by the situation. How could this be possible? And what would this do to his ability to write? I was so flustered I couldn't think of a single thing to say and I lost my chance to tell him how much his books meant to me.

I later learned that, like Beethoven after losing his hearing, he would continue delighting his fans with the products of his imagination. He went on to finish his Cadwal Chronicles and three more SF novels.

I also learned at Magicon about the special relationship between Underwood-Miller publishers and Vance. I subscribed to their notices and so began to buy their hardback editions of his novels. Even after the

---

✸ *Dan Temianka collected, and Underwood-Miller published in 1992, a whopping (and most entertaining) compendium of about 1700 "coined words" in Jack Vance's works.*

*partnership dissolved, Chuck Miller continued to mail out a flyer where he offered used copies of Vance books. This way I was able to read his crime and mystery novels, like **The Man in the Cage** and **Bird Island**.*

And so, bits and pieces, my Jack Vance collection grew to completion. Examining the scope of his work, I am struck by the effort he spent in the little details that bring to life his creations. For example, when he describes the notorious smell in the town of Yipton, he even gives it a name and a recipe:

The Big Chife - a tentative recipe
(Araminta Station; II, 9)

Ingredient	Parts per 100
Human exudations	25
Smoke and charred bones	8
Fish, fresh	1
Fish, rotten	8
Decaying coral (very bad)	20
Canal stink	15
Dexax	8
Complex cacodyls	13
Unguessable (bad)	2

Vance seems to enjoy coming up with fantastical, unusual names in his stories. Here are other lists that you might find interesting, but with a twist. Each of the following lists has a single entry that is not part of the group; your task is to figure out <u>which one doesn't belong</u>. The answers are in the last page of this chapter.

You may wish to start with "The Big Chife" above, however, as one of the ingredients is incorrect!

Vissel River Showboats
(Showboat World)

Phoebus
Fironzelle's Golden Conceit
Psychopompos Revenant
Pamellissa
Two Varminies
Universal Panconium

The Naturalists Societies
(The Book of Dreams; XV)

Friends of Nature
Leave Be
Exemplary Corps
Life in God Church
Sierra Club
Women for Natural Procreation

The Castles of Old Earth
(The Last Castle)

Delora
Sea Island
Maraval
Haidion
Morninglight
Janeil
Hagedorn

Sirene instruments
(The Moon Moth)

hymerkin
strapan
krodatch
double-kamanthil
aquaclave
slobo

How are you doing so far?

"Gentlemen, I feared from the very first that it might come to this. Mind you, I hoped and proposed possibilities to myself; I weighed this against that even as we sat talking. Always I reverted to the bitter facts. Lonas, where has your thinking taken you?"

"The facts are bitter." (Araminta Station; VII, 3)

Well, let's continue with the lists:

The Eight Arch-magicians of the Elder Isles
(Suldrun's Garden; X)

Baibalides
Coddefut
Desmëi
Iucounu
Murgen
Myolander
Noumique
Widdefut

Hussade traditional orchestral compositions
(Trullion: Alastor 2262; XIV, XV)

The Great Games at Woon Winday
Moods of Sheirl Hralce
Glory of Forgotten Heroes
Marvels of Grace and Glory
Sheirls Softly Hopeful for Glory
Scintillating Glorifications

Languages of the Paonese People
(The Languages of Pao)

Cogitant
Valiant
Technicant
Mercantil
Pastiche

Sirene masks
(The Moon Moth)

Forest Goblin
Thunder Goblin
Sea-Dragon conqueror
Moon Moth
Chalekun
Tanchinaro

The Dragons of Aerlith
(The Dragon Masters)

Blue horror
Fiend
Jugger
Long-horned murderer
Mermelant
Spider
Striding murderer
Termagant

And now it's time to check your answers in the next page.

The Big Chife –**dexax** *is the explosive contained in the torcs by which the Faceless Man controlled the people (The Anome). The missing ingredient is* **Dry fronds, mats, bamboo** *for 8%.*

Vissel River showboats– **Phoebus** *is the name of the touring ship in Space Opera. The list could have included any of the following:* **Miralda's Enchantment, Vissel Dominator, Melodious Hour, Voyuz, Star-wisp, Perfumed Oliolus, Empyrian Wanderer** *or* **Fireglass Prism.**

Naturalists Societies – **Exemplary Corps** *were the men who fought to defend King Kragen in The Blue World. Missing societies are* **Scutinary Vitalists** *and* **Biological Falange**.

The Castles of Old Earth – **Haidion** *is the name of King Casmir's castle in Suldrun's Garden.* **Alume, Halcyon** *or* **Tuang** *are acceptable substitutes.*

Sirene instruments – **Aquaclave** *is a musical instrument mentioned in Where Hesperus Falls. The* **ganga, zachinko, kiv, gomapard, stimic, skaranyi** *and the* **crebarin** *are additional Sirene instruments.*

Arch-Magicians of the Elder Isles – **Iucounu**, *the "laughing magician", propels Cugel's adventures.* **Sartzanek** *is the eighth name.*

Hussade traditional orchestral compositions – **The Great Games at Woon Winday** *is an entry in Howard Alan Treesong's The Book of Dreams.* **War Song of the Miraksian Players** *is an acceptable answer.*

Languages of Pao – **Mercantil** *is the language of a nearby trading world.* **Paonese**, *as the original language of Pao, was missing from the list.*

Sirene masks – *The* **Tanchinaro** *mask was worn by the Hussade team of the same name in Trullion: Alastor 2262. The list is completed by any of the following:* **Tarn-Bird, Fire-snake, Cave Owl, Wise Arbitrer, Equatorial Serpent, Alk-Islander, Shark-God, Red-bird, Green-bird, Waldemar, Universal Expert, Sand Tiger, Dragon-Tamer, Sophist Abstraction, Black Intricate, Star-wanderer, Prince Intrepid, Seavain, South-Wind, Gay Companion, Emerald Mountain, Triple Phoenix** *or* **Bright Sky Bird.**

The Dragons of Aerlith – *The* **Mermelant** *is an animal used for drayage in Cugel's Saga. The only Dragon missing is, of course the* **Basic**.

So how did you do? If these questions seemed difficult, do not despair; after all…

"You still have your life. You stand before me, you breathe, your blood flows, you radiate life and beauty."

"That is how a Monster might justify his crime."

"You suggest that I am a Monster, that I took your vitality?"

"I made no such accusation; I commented on the style of your thinking."

"Then I shall refrain from thinking," said Waylock. (To Live Forever; VII, 1)

"Throw away the cork"

Chapter Twelve

Let's see... have I forgotten anything?

"Sometimes, Glawen, I find you absolutely unpredictable. Haven't you forgotten something?"
Glawen paused and gazed dreamily out over the water. "I can't think of anything. Of course, if I'd forgotten it, that's what one would expect." (Araminta Station; I, 1)

Ah yes! I've neglected to explain how this book came into being!

" Do you care to hear the particulars?"
"Yes, within limits imposed by brevity and pertinence." (Throy; II, 4)

As I grow older I've realized that my tastes in Science Fiction and Fantasy have changed somewhat. Although the current trend seems to be to publish books of 400+ pages, I am no longer content to read them just to keep my mind occupied. Many of these thick books are full of "filler" (endless descriptions and long monologues that do not advance the story – or worse, entertain!).

"What basis do you have for these remarks?"
"Popular rumor."
Palafox smiled thinly. "And if by chance you could verify these rumors, what then?"
Beran forced himself to stare into the obsidian gaze. "Your question has no application. It refers to a situation already of the past."
"Your meaning is obscure." (The Languages of Pao; XVIII)

*Thankfully some of these newer long works did capture my imagination and kept me entertained, such as Neil Gaiman's **Neverwhere** and the **Harry Potter** series. Still, I found myself going back to read many of the old books I kept through the years, as if visiting old friends.*

In 1998 my son Javi began to play collectible card games (Wizards of the Coast's Magic: the Gathering being the most

popular), in particular the Star Wars CCG. On Thursday nights I would drive him to a not-so-local Comics store, where he would play for hours. I had to stick around for him to finish and, to while away the time, I would bring a book to read.

One of those evenings I brought a Vance book and, being amused by a particularly entertaining passage, I marked the page so as to be able to find it later. Then I did it again, and then once more.

"It seems a most elaborate procedure," Hilyer grumbled. "Do you have a goal in view? Or will you be satisfied with the first hare to leap from the thicket?" (Night Lamp; IV, 5)

After going through several books, marking those passages, I realized how entertaining it might be to put together a book of such excerpts; this was the beginning of my project. If nothing else, it would "force" me to re-read every Vance book - a task to be enjoyed.

But would loyal and discriminating Jack Vance fans take kindly to such a project?

"Do you consider this social conduct?"
Amiante asked mildly, "Is it irregulationary?"
"It is certainly bumptious and improper! You mock an august office! Many people will be disturbed and distracted!" (Emphyrio; IX)

Whether I could meaningfully present this material might come into question, but

"I have a profound admiration for myself," said Twisk. "Is this vanity? The point is debatable." (Madouc; VIII, 3)

"Interesting," said Hidders. "You have the gift of expressing complicated ideas in simple language. And now?" (Big Planet; I)

The next question was how to get permission to publish this book. Patrick Dusoulier, who hosts the Jack Vance message board on yuku.com, made this possible. He is an expert on all things Vancian so I approached him with no little trepidation. I did not want to seem presumptuous; after all,

A moment's lapse, a tactless remark, an absent-minded glance might negate months of striving. To presume to a status one had not earned was met with instant rebuff. The perpetrator would incur wondering contempt, and might well be branded a 'schmeltzer'.❦ (Night Lamp; II, 1)

❦ Schmeltzer: one who attempts to ingratiate himself, or mingle, with individuals of a social class superior to his own.

Patrick not only allowed me to contact Mr. John Vance (the author's son), but also kindly gave me permission to use the passages and quotes he and some friends had collected a few years back. I would now like to express my deepest appreciation to him.
Was it easy then to contact John Vance?

"Who is calling? Doctor who?"
"Dr. Aartemus, of Narghuys Medical Sciences. I'd like a word with Dr. Leuvil."
"Is he expecting a call from you?"
"I think not; however - "
"You are an old friend?"
"I think not; however - "
"Then Dr. Leuvil will not speak with you."
"Surely this is most surly of him! I am a colleague - neither a bill collector nor a charity patient!" (Frietzke's Turn; VIII)

And when I was finally able to send him a proposal letter, this was his response:

"You're either crazy - or so utterly impertinent as to amount to the same thing."
"Not at all," said Jean. "I'm very courteous. There might be a difference of opinion, but still it doesn't make you automatically right." (Abercrombie Station; V)

NOT TRUE! Mr. Vance was most friendly and kind. He thought it was a good idea, then forwarded my request to his father's agent.
Was it easy then to contact the agent?

"At the moment I want a few words with Visbhume. You saw him last night; where is he now?"
Tamurello smilingly shook his head. "He went his way, I went mine; I know nothing of his present locality."
"Why not alter the habits of a lifetime and speak with candor?" asked Shimrod. "Truth, after all, need not be only the tactic of last resort." (The Green Pearl; XVII, 2)

Since I didn't hear from the agent, I wrote back to John, who counseled patience.

"Be patient," said Gersen. "We are making our decision."
The remark annoyed the woman. Her voice took on a coarse edge. " 'Be patient,' you say? All night I pour beer for crapulous men; isn't that patience enough? Come over here, backwards; I'll put this spigot somewhere amazing, at full gush, and then we'll decide who calls for patience!" (The Face; III)

69

After waiting for a few more months I finally received an answer. He gave me approval to do a limited run of 1,000 copies with certain conditions.

"Do I make myself clear? Trewan?"
Trewan spoke in a surly voice: "I shall obey, of course. Still, I was under the impression - "
"Revise that impression." (Suldrun's Garden; VIII*)*

The most important condition, and the one that most mattered to me, was that Mr. Vance would have final say on whether to allow the publishing of the book as written. I most certainly didn't want to offend my literary hero. And besides, I didn't want to face a guilty verdict of slander!

"Therefore, Sir Guyal, though loath, I am forced to believe you guilty of impertinence, impiety, disregard and impudicity. Therefore, as Castellan and Sargeant-Reader of the Litany, responsible for the detention of lawbreakers, I must order you secured, contained, pent, incarcerated and confined until such time as the penalties will be exacted." (The Dying Earth: Guyal of Sfere)

Myron nodded thoughtfully. "Someday I will calculate what his statement cost him per syllable. A really exorbitant amount, when you think of it. After all, a syllable when spoken by itself conveys no meaning. If Hatchkey had separated his comment into syllables, then had read the list to the judge from bottom to top, the judge would have found no offense, and might have let Hatchkey off with only a warning." (Ports of Call; I, 2)

Once I agreed then I received by mail the contract, to be signed in duplicate.

"Is all this clear?"
"You speak with authority! I must accept your concepts."
(Throy; VIII, 4)

And so this book was written.

"Now, Farr Sainh, may I ask an impertinent question?"
"One more won't hurt me." (The Houses of Iszm; II)

Yes, I'm sure I haven't included every single memorable passage or quote from Vance's books. Perhaps I haven't even included your favorite one! I would ask, kind reader, that you help the Vancian fan community by contributing your own favorites. To do so, please log onto my website www.lugoeye.com, then go into the "books" section and post your favorites.

And now that it's finished, let's break the champagne!

Yamb gave a hacking cough. "Ah, my poor throat - dry as rusk! Woman, have we no tipsic to drink? Is not life to be lived as a glorious adventure, with tipsic to be shared among good friends? Or must we whimper and tiptoe around all the good things, proud only of our frugal austerity? We cannot drink tipsic once we are dead! Bring out the bottle, woman! Pour with a loose wrist and an eager hand! This is a great day!" (Night Lamp; XV, 3)

"Drink, Professor Kutte, then play! As you never have played before!'

Director Kutte bowed stiffly and pushed aside the proffered flasks. "Excuse me, I do not drink ferments or spirits. Teaching expressively condemns their use."

"Bah! Tonight we throw a blanket over theology, as we might cover a cantankerous parrot. Let us rejoice! Drink, Professor!" (The Book of Dreams; XIII)

Chilke refilled the goblets and signaled to the steward.

"Yes sir?"

"Another jug of Blue Ruin. We are about to get serious so throw away the cork." (Throy; III, 1)

October 18, 2010

Maitland, FL

71

Made in the USA
Monee, IL
04 January 2021